Alberta Clipper

John Salter

Livingston Press
at the University of West Alabama

ISBN 0-942979-88-5, clothbound
ISBN 0-942979-89-3, quality paper

Library of Congress Catalogue # 2001099094

Printed on paper that meets or exceeds the acid content
requirements of the Library of Congress

Printed in the United States by:
Cloth binding by: Heckman Bindery

Cover Photo: James R. Dean

Cover design: Joe Taylor

Proofreading: Julian Tyler, Terri Barbour, Beau Beaudreaux,
Jodie Hightower, Suzanne Knight, Robin Allen,
Heather Loper, Ariane Godfrey

Acknowledgements:
These stories appeared, in slightly different form,
in the following publications:
"Shoshone Insurance," in *Nebraska Review*;
"Barley," in *Massachusetts Review*;
"Big Ranch," in *Third Coast* and *Best American Mystery Stories 2001*;
"Scorpions," in *Washington Review*;
"Sea-Mist," in *Parting Gifts*;
"Three Drum Theories," in *North Dakota Quarterly*;
"The Bear's Fourth Leg," in *Florida Review*,
and "Experience With Ravens," in *Pearl*.

First edition
5 4 3 2 1

TABLE OF CONTENTS

For Nancy,
Who kept it going.

Shoshone Insurance

I didn't take Jack Sample's watch. That would be crazy. Walk around with a dead man's watch. It wasn't no Rolex but it did have a chunky gold band that anyone could spot. The law would have seen it was missing if they found him. Jack's arms was dark, from the sun, but under the watch his skin was white. Like his legs.

Hannah, she wanted the watch, but I told her no. If this was Sacramento, maybe, or Reno. But not up in the woods. People would notice. "It don't matter," she said. "I'm dying anyway."

"No," I told her. "You're only a dying a little at a time. Could be years."

Old Jack, he was on his stomach, on Hannah's bed. Buck ass naked. Still looking at the window like he was when I come through it with the bat. I put the watch back on his arm. I had trouble with the clasp. It went this way and that way. "It's backwards," Hannah said.

"What's backwards?" I asked her.

"The watch. The time part. Upside down or whatever."

I went to fix but she grabbed my arm. "Leave it," she said. She started laughing. She started laughing but it was her crazy laugh and in a minute it changed over to crying.

I didn't take Jack's watch but I took his money. Four hundred bucks. All arranged, small bills first. All the presidents facing the same way like they just come out of the cash register. Money was different than a watch. It could spread out, like dead water when you throw in a rock.

I messed it up before I put it in my pocket. I had plans for that money. Give some to Hannah, for little Charlie, and use the rest to get up to Arcata. In prison a guy from Humboldt State came down to visit some of us in the art program. Said he could fix me up with a place to sleep. Study art up there. This guy did time himself, way back. Told me face to face, said guys like me better not go home after they get done. Said home becomes a prison, prison becomes a home. Something like that.

I almost forgot about Jack's car. Had to be bright red. Parked in front where anyone could see it if they glanced up from the highway. I went out to look it over while Hannah took a bath to wash Jack off her. Mostly I wanted out. Out of the house. Jack dead in there. Hannah crying in the bathtub. I wanted to clear my head.

I lit one of Hannah's Kools and walked around the car. Didn't touch it, just walked around it. All the doors was locked. Fucker locked it up tight. If Hannah had been ready with her money he would have been in and out in five minutes. Maybe less. Might have only stood on the porch while she went for her purse. Might have even let the engine run. Made me think he had it all planned out, driving up Indian Hill. Moving that cinnamon toothpick around in his mouth. Maybe thinking about her long hair, down to her waist, almost. Maybe thinking about more.

Hannah, she kept herself up pretty good even after little Charlie was born. My other sisters sure let theirselves go. All those babies left something behind. Not Hannah. It was softball done it for her. In school she was pitcher for the girl's team. Took them all the way to state her junior year. Me and Gran, we followed the team all over. Down to Chico. Up to Susanville. All over.

Hannah could run, she could bat. Did it all. She could have gotten herself a scholarship but at the end of the season she got caught messing around with Coach. Turned out a lot of people knew what was going on but kept their mouths shut on account of Hannah being so good and Coach being such a nice guy. What happened was Coach's wife drove to Redding to surprise him at a tournament there. The motel guy let her into his room and she found some of Hannah's things. Hannah's underwear and the cream she used for her lupus. If it wasn't for that cream, Coach could have maybe lied, but his wife, she found the tube, found where some of it had rubbed off on the sheet. That's what they said, anyway. The school didn't fire Coach but he quit. Someone told me he was working over to Elko, not coaching no more but working in a casino. His wife moved away, back to Iowa or somewhere like that. Hannah dropped out.

She kept playing softball for awhile. On the county leagues, on the all girls teams. Hannah run her team like it was the army for a couple of years. No beer until afterwards. No swearing. Then her lupus got worse and she didn't want to go outside no more, at least not on sunny days. The doctor told her it was okay as long as she wore the cream and long sleeves, but she didn't want to risk it. She didn't want to leave little Charlie alone.

That's who she got the insurance for. Little Charlie. I was there when Jack sold it to her, back before I went down to Oroville and got in trouble. Jack got Hannah's name off her doctor, he said. Come over to the house and set her down at the table, told her how the insurance worked, how little Charlie would get this pile of money if anything ever happened to her. Hannah said she couldn't afford it and Jack, he just pointed at the couch where me and little Charlie was sitting and watching cartoons. "That little fellow like to eat hamburgers?" he asked.

"Yes," Hannah said.

"You ever take that little fellow uptown to the drive-in?"

"Sometimes," Hannah said.

"And french fries? Growing boy like that must like his french fries. Probably a milkshake, too, once in awhile."

"Sometimes."

"Well," Jack said. "You skip the drive-in once a month, you can afford a good life policy. I bet you can do that."

Shoshone Insurance, his card said. Jack Sample. He wasn't no Shoshone. Maybe a Paiute, I told Hannah. She laughed. She was feeling better after I took and hauled Jack out to the car, and moved the car up behind the shed and covered it with the wood tarp. Anyone messing around back there would have found it, but it was still broad daylight and the best I could do.

I threw the card in the woodstove and watched it catch around the edges and disappear. "What about his wallet?" Hannah asked.

"Burn it," I told her. "Got to burn everything."

"No," she said. "It'll stink up the house. It'll stink worse than the credit cards. I'll throw up." She rolled onto her back, on the rug. She opened the wallet and put it across her chest, over her bra. "Check it out," she said.

"Give it to me," I said. "Quit fooling around like that."

I put the wallet in Jack's briefcase and rolled the locks. We burned everything else. All his forms. All the money orders and checks. A lot of people had Shoshone insurance. There was some white names from Okie Flats but mostly it was people. Uncle Bunny, the twins. All our relations. "Milo," she said. "He don't need no insurance. He ain't dying."

"He works in the woods," I said. "He's a faller. He could get killed pretty easy out there."

Shoshone Insurance

"But it's not for sure. Not like me."

"You're not for sure," I said. "Aunty Pat has lupus and she's old."

"Marion died when she was twenty-six. Don't tell me it's not for sure. I got it worse than Pat anyhow." She sat up. "Put my cream on for me. On my back."

"I got things to do," I said. "I got to figure out what to do with Jack."

"Please, Donald," she said. She handed me the tube. I never liked the way it smelled. She took off her bra and laid down again on her stomach. I rubbed some on her back. I could feel her relax under my hand. "Lower," she said.

"Why?" I asked her. "You never go outside anyway."

"Lower," she said. "Rub it in all over."

Hannah got strange with the lupus. Maybe she was already strange. When I was in prison she came down to visit me once. Sat across from me and we talked through the glass. About home. About little Charlie. How he wasn't taking after Coach at all. How he took after our side. In the middle of talking, Hannah unsnapped her shirt. She had on a western shirt with pearl snaps and she just opened it up. She wasn't wearing no bra. She grabbed her boobs and pointed them at me "Take a look," she said. "You can think about them if you want."

Later on, she snuck me some pictures. Polaroid pictures of herself without no clothes on. I never knew who took them. I kept them stashed most of the time. Once in a while I loaned them out, like for cigarettes. I had to trade one of them for a knife when I thought I was going to have to take care of this guy. Someone else took care of him for me. I never told nobody Hannah was my sister. "Man," they'd say. "Your old lady is fucking hot. I bet you're going crazy thinking about her."

I used the pictures once to make a drawing of Hannah. Took me a week. It turned out good. I made her traditional, with a basket hat. The guy from up at Humboldt State liked it. He bought it off me, said he was going to hang it in the Indian club up there.

Around midnight I drove Jack up to Crystal Lake. The idea come to me in a dream when me and Hannah fell asleep by the woodstove. I remembered Grampa telling me how back in the fifties, some guys from the state came up to try and measure how deep Crystal Lake was. They hired Grampa to be their helper, went out on a boat and screwed these metal rods together. "They come back all bent," Grampa told me. "All bent from the pressure." I never did know if the story was true but I heard about this gold miner down around Taylorsville was digging a shaft against Mount Hough, and everyone thought he'd drill into the bottom of Crystal and wash the town away. I thought, *must be deep if they all tell these stories about it.* Plus I knew there wasn't going to be nobody up there and I knew the way in the dark.

Hannah, she wanted to come along. "The stars will be big up there," she said. "We can climb up in the fire tower and look at the stars."

"There won't be time for no stars," I told her. "This will take me all night because I got to walk back down and not get seen by nobody."

"It's my fault he got himself killed," she said. "I should take him up there."

"It's not your fault," I told her. "It's his fault for making you give it up. It's my fault for having a bad temper. That's how you got to look at it. You didn't do nothing."

I never meant to hit Jack so hard. But when I come back from town and seen his car there, when I looked in the window, something just went to fire in me, like it did in Oroville when I got in trouble there. We was drinking in a park and an off-duty cop got in my face. Told us to leave the park for families. Next thing I know, his jaw is broke and they're pushing my face in the cement, in the parking lot. Rubbed the skin off my cheek so now it's all light colored there, all scar tissue.

It took me a long time to get up to Crystal. All dirt, all the way. Places you could drop off and fall forever. The other times I went up there, we was drunk and in a hurry and it didn't matter because we didn't think about getting killed or caught. But with Jack it took me forever because I turned off all the lights and drove with just the moon.

Up on top there's a little campground where we used to party, and another road that goes down to the lake. Cuts almost straight down, sharp, down to the water. The lake isn't very big. You could throw a rock all the way across.

When I got up there I didn't know what to do. I parked on the hill and looked down at the lake. Lit a smoke and sat there with Jack. Sat there in the dark with Jack. He wasn't puffing up that I could tell and didn't stink yet but I didn't like being with him. Not on account of ghosts or nothing. I just didn't like it. I was thinking

Shoshone Insurance

too much. Got to wondering if she offered it to him. Maybe she paid him that way every time. Got lonely, maybe, so that even an old guy like Jack looked good. She never went out no more.

I didn't put Jack in the driver's seat like I thought I would. I got in a hurry. In the movies, they always put a brick on the gas pedal but I had the hill for speed. I just put the car in gear and let it go.

I watched it. I watched it go down the hill, crunching on the gravel. When it got to the bottom and hit the sand, it started to slow down. I thought it might bog down but it went in. Kind of coasted out a ways. Floated. It didn't sink right off. Just sat there in the water, kind of turning around like an old board would. I didn't want to see it go under. I walked down the hill, down to the sand, and kicked around at the tracks so nobody would ever know it went in. I heard it start to go. Crystal is surrounded by rocks. These cliffs. Made it loud as hell. We used to scream down there and the sound would get bigger and bigger, traveling around the rocks.

I seen the future once at Crystal Lake. Not by the water but up near the campground. We was drinking and I went off by myself, over to the edge. I could see the road way down there. I seen a logging truck trying to pass an old pickup. I thought it was too close to the curve but those guys won't slow down for nothing. They get paid by the load, by the board foot. From up high I seen a car coming the other way. I knew what was going to happen. I knew they was going to go head-on. Nobody knew it but me. Couldn't do nothing about it. Just watched it happen. I sat there for a long time, seen the highway patrol come out, seen the ambulance. Seen these tiny people running around. Two people got killed in that wreck. The dentist's wife and their baby. I never told nobody what I seen.

The law, they showed up sooner than I thought they would. Put Jack in the lake on Monday and on Wednesday morning we looked out and seen a patrol car coming. Hannah, she didn't understand. "How do they know?" she asked.

"They know you had the insurance," I told her. "They got records. They got a trail to follow."

"Fuck," she said.

"Just be cool," I told her.

"I'll lie," she said. "Say he never did come over that day."

"No," I said. "You got to think. Someone might have seen his car up here. They'll trip you up. Say as much truth as you can. Say you paid him cash like always. Say you don't know where he went after that."

"I'm a good liar," she said.

I wanted to ask if she lied to me about Jack but there wasn't no more time and I didn't want her to get upset and blow it. The patrol car was in the yard by then. It was Deputy Hill. I never liked him. Walked around all bad-ass because he lifted weights. Had arms like you never seen. All the time hassling people.

I went through the window. Same window in the bedroom I come through to get Jack. I thought about taking off right then. I still had the money in my pocket. But I wanted to hear what she said. She fucked up and my plans would have changed.

They was in the kitchen at first so I couldn't hear good. Heard Hill walking around, making the whole floor creak, probably poking around like cops do, looking at everything. Touching everything. Then I heard Hill laugh. Heard Hannah laugh. I didn't know what they was laughing at. What could have been so funny, looking for a man missing, maybe dead for all Hill knew. I just leaned against the house, hearing them talk but not really hearing the words, and then I seen the future again. Not like up at Crystal that time but in my head. Seen it play out in my head, knew what was going to happen even before they went into the bedroom.

I should have taken off right then. Run into town, hitch a ride over to Redding and catch a bus up north. Don't know why I stayed, because I knew what was going to happen. I heard them. Heard Hannah say, "Let me do that," and then Hill's gun belt was hanging over the window sill, close enough that I could smell the leather. Made me sick, that smell, all heavy, worse than Jack's wallet. Then I heard the bed springs press down.

I couldn't help but look, peek in from the corner. Seen Hill's back, all cut and hard from the weights. Hannah's legs was wrapped around him. She had the watch on her ankle. Jack's watch, digging into Hill's back. I never knew she took it off Jack. I seen Hannah's face over Hill's shoulder. Her eyes was wide open. "Do it," she whispered.

"Baby," Hill said.

"Do it," she said again. Hill just grunted. He was so big Hannah just about disappeared under him. "Do it," she said. She was talking to me. My chin was right near his gun belt. I could smell his gun, smell that oil. Hannah, she bit her lip while he was going at it. The bed was slamming around, kind of walking around the room. "Please," she said. She licked Hill's shoulder. I waited for the fire to take hold in me but it didn't. It didn't because this time I wasn't taken by surprise like those other times. I already knew what was going to happen. Hannah started to cry. "Do it," she kept saying. She made her finger like a gun and pressed it against Hill's head. He didn't have a clue. Just kept pounding on her. His back was getting shiny from sweat. I heard those springs screaming, smelled the leather, smelled the gun, heard Hannah saying *do it do it do it,* when I backed off from the window and headed for the trees, headed for Arcata.

John Salter

THREE DRUM THEORIES

Smoky was wide awake when the drumming began. It was midnight and he would normally have been asleep, but his left eye was keeping him up. The eye was still sore after a freak accident earlier in the evening, when Volney and Linda Vincent were over. Right after dinner, Volney had produced a joint, handing it to Linda on his way to the kitchen for more Chardonnay. Smoky didn't like marijuana because it made him feel paranoid, but believed in being a good host, and from his perch on the floor had lit a match for Linda. When she'd bent to the flame, the crystal she wore on a thong around her neck swung out and struck Smoky's eye. The crystal was huge, jagged, fresh from being recharged in Sedona. Smoky had jerked in reflex, knocking the joint into his wine glass, ruining it at least for the short term. There had been some tension, then, with Volney upset about his joint and Linda worried about Smoky's eye. It had watered for some time.

Thump, thump thump. The sound, hollow and watery, echoed through the trees and into Smoky's bedroom. His back prickled immediately. *Thump, thump, thump.* He was terrified. He felt as if the sound was pressing him against the mattress, squeezing the air from his lungs. His mind whirled. He thought it could only be ghosts from the ancient campground underneath his house. The land developer, foreseeing problems, had brought a Maidu elder up from Oroville to bless each home site. Smoky still had the certificate of reconciliation in his desk, but doubted it would mean much to angry spirits returning home after a century-long journey.

Linda Vincent was in bed, staring over the top of a book at a mole on Volney's back, centered between his bony shoulders. She was thinking about pinching the mole between her thumb and forefinger, about plucking it from her husband like a wood tick. She'd heard that cut moles bled profusely. She pictured Volney's life oozing from the spigot on his back, soaking into their futon, his wet snoring growing fainter and fainter. She closed the book. She would roll up the futon with Volney inside and tie it with nylon cord. She would drag the bundle outside and throw it on the brush pile in the clearing between their house and Smoky's. After the first snow, when there was no danger of igniting the entire forest, she would burn the pile.

She was getting to the part where the flames caught the bundle, flaring wildly, when the drumming began. *Thump, thump, thump*. At first, she thought the sound was in her head. Sometimes, just before falling asleep, she heard voices, snippets of conversation. Completely mundane stuff: "Don't forget the milk," or, "He never said for sure." When she mentioned this to Volney he'd said something about signals, how thoughts traveled across the sky like radio signals and if you were in the right frame of mind, you picked them up. It could happen to anyone, he'd argued. It wasn't a gift.

Thump, thump, thump. When Linda realized it was coming from outside, she turned away from Volney and switched off her reading lamp. She pulled off her glasses and strained to listen. *Thump, thump, thump*. The sound had an ethereal quality to it. Almost mournful, she thought. She sat upright. She felt drawn to the sound. It reminded her of something from *Close Encounters of the Third Kind*. She stood and moved to the open window, arms outstretched, palms facing the night. She would go, gladly, she thought.

Felipe was on patrol, walking the perimeter of his land with a Ruger Mini-14, making one of the twelve complete revolutions he made every night, summer or winter, between midnight and six. He was about a hundred yards from his house, thinking about detouring to make a peanut butter sandwich, when he heard it. *Thump, thump, thump*. It was exactly what he had always imagined a mortar would sound like: deep and powerful, beautifully lethal, like a handmade knife or a well-executed groin kick.

Felipe dropped to the ground and tried to become one with the earth as he waited for incoming rounds. His heart pounded. He clenched his teeth, afraid that his breathing could be heard all the way down to the creek. He was pleased, though, with his reaction time. He was glad he'd been training with ravens, pretending their occasional, throaty calls were gunshots as he worked around the house. The ravens had been very helpful in simulating surprise attacks, although lately he'd been worried that interlopers might catch on and use raven calls to confuse him during a raid.

Thump, thump, thump. Felipe gripped the rifle. He had to go to the bathroom, badly, an issue not addressed in any of the manuals he frequently ordered from advertisements in *Soldier of Fortune*. It was not a mortar, he decided. It was a drum. Their way of signaling, perhaps? Whistles would be too obvious. Radios were not secure. A drum made sense. Who would suspect a drum?

Felipe grinned. The black makeup on his face cracked. He would suspect a drum. He would not be fooled. He would be waiting to cut them to ribbons. Their drumming would be the futile drumming of the British, of the Confederacy, of Custer's troops at Little Bighorn.

Smoky fought back with light. He turned on his bedside lamp, which gave him the courage to wobble into the kitchen and flip the switch. The white floors and counters shone. He was glad that he'd cleaned thoroughly after his dinner with Linda and Volney. A clean kitchen looked brighter, friendlier. Safer. He felt better, but he could still hear the drum. Thump, thump, thump. And when a breeze rustled the woodpile tarp, fresh chills walked his spine.

He lighted a cigarette with shaky hands and drank the rest of the Chardonnay, straight from the bottle. He calmed enough to fix the approximate origin of the sound. It was coming from David Clayton's place. It had to be, Smoky thought, pressing his ear against the sliding screen door. It was definitely coming from upstream and Clayton's was the last site in the development. Beyond, it was all Forest Service land. Clayton owned the best property because the view, at least in theory, would be pristine forever. It was also the most expensive plot for that reason, and out of Smoky's grasp. He'd been forced to settle for the next one down. As it was, Smoky could only see a sliver of Clayton's tiny, redwood-sided A-frame, but it always bothered him, just knowing it was there.

He stepped out to the deck and listened. *Thump, thump, thump.* The pattern didn't vary. Triple thump, long pause, triple thump. Smoky followed the beat for a few moments, waving his cigarette like a conductor's baton. He felt giddy, now, after his initial fear. Even if it had been ghosts, he decided, they would no doubt be friendly to him. They'd know he was okay. He always tried to do

Three Drum Theories

the right things. Whenever he thinned trees, he apologized to the earth before biting in with his chainsaw. He tried to help the local Maidu people in realistic, non-patronizing ways. He always bought Indian tacos from their booth at the county fair, even though fried bread was obscenely high in cholesterol.

The drumming was still a mystery, though. Who would pound a drum at midnight? Musicians, of course. Maybe Indians, or at least self-proclaimed Indians, like Oglala Bob, who wore fringed buckskin boots and published a newsletter, and sold automobile prayer flags at craft fairs. The prayer flags were tiny shreds of cloth meant to be tied to radio antennas. They were supposed to repel deer more effectively than bumper mounted whistles. Smoky was pretty sure Oglala Bob would have some sort of drum.

But David Clayton was not a musician, and he'd never claimed to be even part Indian. Clayton didn't sport a ponytail or a silver and turquoise watchband. Smoky could not even recall ever seeing Clayton at the Indian Days festival, which drew a healthy crowd every fall. Actually, he suspected Clayton of being a possible racist. Their mail sometimes got mixed up and Smoky had seen, more than once, envelopes bearing Idaho postmarks. Wasn't Idaho a haven for Nazis?

Smoky leaned over the deck railing and looked toward Clayton's place. It was dark. Was Clayton drunk? It did not seem likely. Clayton seemed pretty straight. Smoky thought he might even be a recovering alcoholic. At the last Willow Creek Land Association meeting, Clayton had sipped Tab instead of wine. Besides, Smoky thought, the beat was too consistent. Thump, thump, thump. Regular as a metronome. Maybe Clayton had gone crazy. Crazy from living alone? Smoky could see that happening. He tended to get a bit squirrelly himself when he went too long without seeing people. It was one of the reasons he had dinner with Volney and Linda the first Thursday of every month. That and the fact that Volney and Linda had no children to worry about. His other friends had to make complicated arrangements with babysitters and were almost always late, something that irritated Smoky since he tended to prepare meals for which timing was important.

Clayton wasn't a hermit, a recluse like Felipe Larson, though. Smoky could see Felipe going nuts and pounding on a drum, but not a man like Clayton. Clayton was your basic retiree, up from the city. Oakland, Smoky thought it was, or maybe Stockton. He thought Clayton had been a high school teacher or a guidance counselor. For awhile, after Clayton moved up to the valley, a rumor was going around that he was a mining engineer, intent on scalping the mountains for industrial gold. Someone had seen him driving around the valley with what appeared to be surveying equipment in his back seat. There'd been an emergency meeting of the Willow Creek Integrity Committee to plan a strategy. Volney had wanted to plant white crosses in Clayton's yard, à la *The Milagro Beanfield War*. But it had turned out to be a false alarm. The surveying equipment was only a camera tripod. Clayton, they'd learned, was an amateur photographer, interested in birds.

Linda leaned from the bedroom window and peered up at the sky. There were no lights. No ship hovered above the house. But she could still hear the sound. *Thump, thump, thump*. She wanted to give herself to the sound, tune in to it completely, but Volney's snoring was distracting her. She tried to tune him out but couldn't. She was filling with negative energy, she realized. That couldn't be very helpful. She whirled around to shake Volney, but stopped short of touching him. Instead, she slid the window shut and hurried past the futon and out the front door.

Thump, thump, thump. Linda sat on the porch, cross-legged, fingering her crystal. She was naked and the night was cool, but she felt a great warmth as if the drumming carried with it some heat. It was not an alien ship, she decided. At least it wasn't coming from the sky. It seemed to be coming from across the clearing. Not from Smoky's place but farther up. David Clayton's place?

She shrugged. If David Clayton wanted to drum, even at midnight, it was okay with her. It was typical of Volney, she decided, not to hear it. When they'd gone to New Orleans, for the blues and gumbo, there'd been a terrible fight in the motel, in the next room. From what she'd gathered, cupping her ear to the wall, someone had gotten caught shacking up with someone else's wife. The husband had actually pounded on her and Volney's door before finding the right room. Volney had slept soundly through it all.

"New Orleans," she whispered. "Key West. Montreal. Churchill, Manitoba. Glacier National Park. Yellowstone. Yosemite." They were all places she'd been with Volney. She chanted them sometimes, when driving in bad weather or on

Three Drum Theories

long hikes. "Denver," she said. "Durango. Isle Royale. Vancouver. Acapulco."

Thump, thump, thump. The sound seemed to be finding her, navigating the trees to bounce against her bare skin. Strange, she thought, leaning back on her elbows, closing her eyes. She felt like she was tied, umbilically, to the drum. The source. Mother's blood. She parted her knees slightly. She wondered if a baby's heartbeat, from the womb, sounded watery, echoed like the drumbeats she was hearing. She had no idea. Once, she'd accompanied a pregnant student to her OB appointment. The doctor had run a probe over Anna's taut belly while an antiquated speaker screeched from a metal table. "There. There it is," the OB had finally said. Anna had wept, in joy or relief, and Linda had dutifully squeezed her hand. But she'd been unable to recognize anything like a heartbeat in the static.

Thump, thump, thump. She'd gotten pregnant once, though, with Volney. It had happened ten years earlier, during a thunderstorm in the Wind River Range. They'd forgotten to pack her birth control pills but after being cooped up in the tent playing cards for hours, they'd given in, not so much to lust as to boredom. Then, just minutes afterward, the sky had abruptly cleared. She hadn't known she was pregnant until they were back home and she miscarried in front of her archaeology class.

"Aspen," she whispered. "Park City. Vail." Who needed children, she always said when she sensed the question forming in someone's mind, with Volney to take care of? Of course, they always thought she and Volney couldn't conceive, even after she found the perfect shirt at a lesbian bookstore in San Jose. On the shirt, a cartoonish Donna Reed sort of woman was biting her hand and looking completely exasperated. "Oh my God, I forgot to have children," the woman was thinking.

Thump, thump, thump. She wondered if David Clayton had children. Probably, she decided. She thought he'd mentioned having a daughter in Idaho once. He probably even had grandchildren. He carried himself like a father. She'd seen him in the grocery store, moving purposefully up and down the aisles. He always seemed very efficient. Not like Volney. Volney explored. Played football with the bread. Stole cherries and hid the pits behind the canned goods. After the miscarriage, he'd said, "One more hand of rummy and it never would have happened."

John Salter

Felipe watched his house intently. He was looking for shadows, flashlights, the glint of their knives in the moonlight, any indication they'd made entry. The drumming was still going strong. *Thump, thump, thump.* Maybe it was meant to distract him, he thought. Maybe they'd already gotten inside. He pictured them floating through the house. Trespassing on his property. Touching his things, reading his logbook. He trembled. He wove his left arm through the rifle sling and took a bead on the window. "Surprise, surprise," he whispered. He flicked off the safety and curled his finger around the trigger.

He did not shoot. It occurred to him that he might still be inside. He might be sleeping soundly. Felipe with the rifle might only be his soul. His body could still be in the house. This had happened before.

"Stop," he said. "Evaluate." He removed his right hand from the rifle and laid it carefully, palm down, on the ground. "No mistakes," he whispered. He put the safety back on with his left hand and sat up. He brought the rifle to his shoulder and peered through the scope, panning across the trees for anything unusual. Smoky's kitchen window flashed by. Felipe found it again and tried to hold for a better look but his arms wobbled and the window danced wildly in the crosshairs. He planted his elbows on his thighs. It was not much better that way but he caught a glimpse of Smoky's face, saw him sucking on a bottle of wine. Felipe took a deep breath, let some of it out, and held the crosshairs on Smoky. "Bang," he whispered.

Thump, thump, thump. Felipe rested the rifle across his legs and closed his eyes. He rotated his head, imagining his ears as radar dishes. Clayton, he thought. The drumming was coming from Clayton's compound. Clayton was one of them. Maybe they weren't attacking, after all. Maybe Clayton had been ordered to drum, to drive him crazy with the sound. Maybe there were subliminal messages in the drumbeats. Maybe he was being programmed even as he sat there, listening. He would have to tune it out. He clapped his hands to his ears. He could still hear it. "La la la," he said. "La la la la la la la."

Water, Smoky thought. Perhaps David Clayton was praying for water. Everyone was. It was beginning to look as if the drought would never end. Earlier in the summer, Smoky had joined several friends atop Mount Ingalls to pray for rain. They had not used a

Three Drum Theories

drum, but everyone joined hands and they'd taken turns asking for help. For rain. They'd chanted, then, one at a time, going around and around the circle, faster and faster. In the middle of it, a single cloud had appeared, hooking itself on the peak, and they'd chanted louder, faster, certain that more clouds would follow to form a thunderhead. But the cloud had evaporated like a soap bubble and they'd all gone home.

That had to be it, Smoky decided. He went back inside. David Clayton was a fly fisherman. He'd complained to Smoky at the last Willow Creek Land Association meeting that he'd spotted Felipe Larson trying to spear fish from the creek. Not only was it against the law, Clayton had said, it was unsportsmanlike.

Smoky rinsed the wine bottle and tossed it into his recycling bin. Yes, he thought. Of course. Fishermen were superstitious as it was. Lucky hats, secret spots. He pictured David Clayton in his back yard, hunkered down by his drum, wrapped in the red wool jacket he always wore when trooping to the convergence with his fly rod and wicker creel. More power to him, he thought.

He crawled into bed and rolled up in his comforter. He listened to the drum. *Thump, thump, thump*. He'd thought he might have to shut the window but now he found the beat soothing. It reminded him of when he was a small boy and his father slipped a pocket watch under his pillow. Now, like the ticking of the watch, the drumbeat nudged him gently toward sleep. One of the pauses widened into a silence. Smoky held his breath. He waited. Please, he thought. Don't stop now. Don't stop now. As if on cue, the drumming resumed, and Smoky began to breath again.

Linda pressed her knees together and rolled onto her side. *Thump, thump, thump*. "Mount Ranier," she said. "Denali. Rocky Mountain National Park. Jackson Hole, Wyoming." They had a photo album for every trip they'd ever taken together. They saved everything. Receipts. Maps. Speeding tickets. They had a Nikon F4 with a motor drive, and a sea kayak that had been in the waters of three countries. She curled into a ball on the porch. She was cold now, but did not want to go inside. *Thump, thump, thump*. She felt the beat against her back, throbbing against her taut skin. "Stop," she whispered. "Stop it." The drumming continued. "White Sands," she said. She hugged her knees. "Monument Valley. Death Valley."

John Salter

Felipe pulled his hands from his ears. No, he thought. That wasn't it. That wasn't it at all. Clayton was warning him. They would come from the north, from the roadless forest, and move past Clayton's place. It was the only logical approach. Clayton must have seen them filing past, on the trail along the creek. That was it. He was sending a warning. The drumming was to warn him. It was all that Clayton, an old man, could really do.

Felipe felt dizzy. He had not known that Clayton cared enough to risk his life. To think he had suspected Clayton. He would have to apologize after the fighting was over. He would have to thank Clayton. They would have to get together to eat and drink wine, like Smoky and the Vincents did every month. Fuck them, he thought. They didn't have a monopoly on friendship along Willow Creek. He shivered. He listened to the drum. *Thump, thump, thump.* "David Clayton," he whispered. "You are my best friend."

David Clayton was surprised that he felt no pain, even with a Ford Crown Victoria resting on his legs. Only his throat was sore, from shouting at the darkness for several hours. And he was cold. The floor of the garage was cold.

Then he'd remembered something. About sound. About the nature of sound, of low frequency sounds in particular. He felt truly blessed that his wrench was still in reach, that the fuel can was nearby. The wrench handle was slick with oil, or blood, or both. But he gripped it tightly and began pounding. Three, he thought. The universal sign of distress. Three gun shots if you were lost while hunting. Three smoky fires. It might take awhile, he decided. But like fishing, patience was the key. Determination. Consistency. The sound, unmistakable in its meaning, would reach the appropriate ears in good time.

Reverse Prototype

Poole and his wife were watching Jay Leno but Poole couldn't follow it. He was thinking about the people next door, Kit and Ellen Loudermilk. He suspected they were having an orgy of some kind. Minutes earlier, when Poole was shutting off the lawn sprinkler in the front yard, a car had pulled into the Loudermilk's driveway. A red sports car. A man and woman had climbed out. Loudermilk had appeared on the porch in a bright yellow Polo shirt and the three of them had shaken hands, talking in low tones, before going into the house.

"So they have company," Poole's wife said. "Big floppy deal. We get company."

"Not like that."

"Like what? So they have a sports car. So what?"

"They carried in luggage."

"So what? People come to stay, they bring luggage."

Poole realized how much he could despise his wife at times. He wanted to squeeze her neck and shout at her like the drill sergeant in *An Officer and a Gentleman*, Bonnie's favorite movie. But he didn't shout. He breathed through his nose for a few moments, calmed down. "They don't know each other."

"Says who?"

"They shook hands."

She dismissed him with a sloppy wave. "You're sick," she said.

He went down to his basement shop, in the furnace room, outfitted with a workbench and vise, an old table saw. When the children—Michael and Lisa—were younger, he'd enjoyed making things, a plywood Santa for the yard, a toy box for their playroom. Now they were gone and he only used the workroom as storage, or to smoke a very occasional cigar when it was forty below outside. It occurred to Poole that anyone listening to his conversations with his wife might assume them to be of retirement age, when in fact Poole was only forty-four. He liked the age, the

John Salter

squareness of the fours. But his birthday was coming up. Forty-five was nothing but a number. He turned on the radio, pressed his palms against the surface of the workbench, stared down at his hands. A week ago he'd held hands with a woman, not his wife. Shirley worked for him. She had the thinnest hair he'd ever seen on a woman, through which her pink scalp glared under the fluorescent lights, and a myriad of fat moles, some extruding hair, on the back of her neck. She was one of those women who never married, who smelled of desperation. He'd caught her once, circling personal ads in the newspaper. How pathetic, he'd thought, how clichéd. They'd gone for lunch, and in a crowd downtown, they'd held hands, not swinging their arms like young lovers but walking close together, elbows locked at their sides. They'd gone to a bar for a sandwich and she'd said, "I love you," just like that. Poole couldn't believe it. "I love you," she'd said. Now he felt weird being around her. She reddened whenever he came near her desk. His secretary, Emily, had reported to Poole that Shirley was "real broken up from the affair." The whole thing had cured him of whatever it was that compelled him to grip her sweaty hand in the first place.

In the middle of the night, Poole woke to urinate. This was a sign of age but not as unwelcome a sign as losing your hair, which he wasn't. Poole didn't look bad, he thought, just a bit weathered. Most women he talked to thought Robert Redford looked better now than in his youth. Clint Eastwood, too, for that matter. Poole had deep spider webs around his eyes and a distinguished touch of gray above his ears. He regarded himself in the bathroom mirror. Smiled. Offered his hand to his reflection. "Bill Poole," he said. "Gotcha. Ten four. Affirmative. Absolutely."

He went downstairs and filled a cup with water and drank it. There were lights on at the Loudermilk's. They'd moved in only the year before. Kit Loudermilk didn't work normal hours. He was some sort of consultant. Poole wasn't sure what he consulted on but he must have been doing well. He frequently unloaded cases of wine from his vintage Mercedes into his house. A bottle had smashed on the driveway once and Poole had watched Loudermilk standing over it for a long time, hand on his hips, staring at the wine as it ebbed down to the street. Later, Mrs. Loudermilk had swept up the mess and curiously, licked pieces of glass before tossing them into the garbage can.

Reverse Prototype

Poole rinsed his cup, shook it dry, placed it upside down on the counter, on a dishtowel. He went to the sliding door facing the deck and opened it, stepped into the night, looked up at the sky. You were supposed to be able to see Venus but he couldn't make out anything different in the torrent of stars. He went to the edge of the deck and peered at the Loudermilk's house. Upstairs lights were on. He thought he heard music. Who were their guests? The couple had seemed just like the Loudermilks—younger, well-off, childless although by choice and not fate, apparently. Loudermilk had talked about children once, as in, *children just wouldn't interface very well with our lifestyle.*

Interface, Poole thought. What kind of interfacing was going on over there? They were up to something. One night, Poole saw Mrs. Loudermilk leaving at ten, dolled up something fierce. Her hair was wild as Medusa's snakes. He'd smelled her perfume, mingled with the aroma of freshly cut grass wafting in from up the street. She'd worn a black cocktail dress as tight around the fanny as those military beds you could supposedly bounce a quarter on. The Loudermilks had kissed on the front steps, a long, passionate kiss, and then she was gone. Early the next morning, when Poole was setting up his ladder to tighten the gutters—an annual task, they always loosened a bit during the winter and caused inefficient flow—Mrs. Loudermilk had returned. She'd looked, frankly, like a rag doll: hair disheveled, pantyhose gone, mascara glopped about her eyes. Carrying her shoes. What could that have been about? He'd waited to hear arguing, loud accusations, but minutes later from his ladder Poole had seen them kissing through the kitchen window. Shocked, he'd been staring, and to his horror Mrs. Loudermilk waved to him before she and Kit disappeared into another room.

Poole went out to the garage, turned on the light, climbed astride his John Deere mower. Bonnie had gotten it for him when he turned forty. He could wipe out the lawn with the Deere in a matter of fifteen minutes or so, although he still used the old push mower to get in close to the shrubbery, and a Weed-eater for along the house and driveway. He rubbed at the green paint with his pajama cuff. He kept the mower spotless. Loudermilk had made a comment when he was washing it in the driveway once: "That's good, wouldn't want to offend the lawn gods." Poole had nodded and laughed but to this day didn't know if he'd been

John Salter

insulted.

How would an orgy like that work, he wondered. Did they all climb into the same bed? Or did they take turns? Draw straws? No, he thought, there weren't enough of them to do that. Maybe they just swapped. Sick, he thought. He looked at his watch. Four-thirty. His nights were not the seamless eight hours of sleep they once were. Not only did he need to get up to urinate, he found himself rising earlier and earlier, and in need of a catnap every afternoon when at work. He'd arranged his schedule so that two to four was what he called research and development time. No phone calls, no interruptions. He was a manager and could do this. He would read trade magazines for awhile, then put his feet up on the desk and take a snooze. Emily would hold off vendors and the store managers with their ridiculous concerns. From four to five he'd leave the office and drop in on a store or two, make suggestions, help set up displays of plastic mugs or deliver supplies if there was a shortage.

Poole climbed off the mower and walked around the garage. He wondered how receptive Bonnie would be to a little early morning fun. Not very, probably. They both had to work in a few hours. Must be nice, he thought, living like the Loudermilks, no morning obligations, plenty of time to drink and screw, like fraternity boys but in a good neighborhood. People talked about the Loudermilks. Ellen Loudermilk liked to sunbathe nude on their deck. She was unabashed. Poole had not seen this but Bonnie had.

He went back into the house, crept up the stairs. Bonnie was stretched out in the bed, occupying the space he'd abandoned. He sat on the edge of the bed and rested his palm on her hip. Her skin was cold. She did not respond to his touch. She was dead to the world. He moved his hand in slow circles. *You have nice hands,* Shirley had said, downtown. *Smooth but strong, like a doctor's hands.* He wondered what Shirley was doing now. Sleeping, he was sure of it. Alone, of course. He imagined she slept with stuffed animals. It occurred to him he could drive over and have sex with her that very minute. He could do that, and be home and mak- for Bonnie before she was even out of h she'd say, appearing in the kitchen with

Poole dressed, slowly, in his jeans an his sneakers. He went downstairs again an His children were off at college, and he v

John Salte

sleeping alone or still up, drinking, talking. He hoped they were having a good time but not too good a time. His own college days had been a laborious five years of working nights, struggling through classes. No partying. No fraternities. Lots of diapers and washing dishes. He'd failed the CPA exam four times before giving up that idea and taking a job with Quade's Pit Stop as an area supervisor. Quade's had over a hundred and ten stores in eleven states and now he was in charge of nineteen of them. They were all basically the same. There were strict guidelines for construction. Prototype and reverse prototype. If you went through the door of a Quade's Pit Stop and the coolers were on the left, it was prototype. On the right, reverse prototype. All the store managers were alike, too. They were all docile. Fear kept them docile. Not fear of Poole or even Quade's, but fear of success. Most of the store managers had college degrees. Liberal arts degrees, mostly, English and History, but a few business degrees. They'd settled. They didn't want to go any further. They couldn't, anyway, not at Quade's. They understood that. In seventeen years Poole had never seen a store manager so much as apply for a headquarters slot. Well, he thought, sipping his coffee, laced heavily with non-dairy creamer. They made their choices. Nobody was holding a gun to their heads, making them waste their education.

He carried his mug out to the yard and stood in his driveway. The grass was wet with dew. Loud birds were bringing in the morning. An occasional car went by, night shift people coming home, young people calling it a night. It was going to be a hot day. Bonnie would be busy at the mall, at the clothing store. They didn't need the money but she liked working there. She liked the discount. He turned and faced Loudermilk's place. Loudermilk rarely spent time on his house but it always seemed neat, the yard adequately trimmed. Ellen Loudermilk would come home after work and mow the lawn quickly when it was needed, not bothering too much with the edges. She wore shorts almost every day. She had a tattoo of a hummingbird on her calf. He imagined her coiled in passion with her husband, and the other couple. What would they talk about before and after? Did they plan, then evaluate the event? Or did they talk about normal things, the Vikings under Dennis Green, or the weather? I'd like to be a fly on the wall at breakfast over there, he thought. Sex? He tried once to talk sexy to Bonnie when they were doing it. "You little slut," he'd said, "you like dirty working men, don't you?" She'd told him to be quiet. She needed to concentrate, she'd said, in order to make the act satisfying. She didn't have much of an imagination, she admitted later. Poole had been embarrassed for her to bring it up because the words had come out of nowhere, had shocked him even as they were forming on his lips.

Loudermilk had invited him over once. They'd been in the yard, just after a thunderstorm, almost a tornado, had ripped through town, snapping limbs, stealing garbage cans and wading pools, cutting power to some areas. In their newer neighborhood the trees were all young and flexible so the damage was minimal. "This is Plasticland," Loudermilk had said. "Snap-together USA. You can't mess this place up." He'd been shirtless, in loose shorts, barefoot, drinking a beer at seven in the morning. His skin was tan all year round. This was not long after Loudermilk had arrived, maybe the first time they'd visited beyond nodding. "You should come over for a drink one of these nights," Kit had said. He'd scratched his hairy chest absent-mindedly. "Come over for a drink with Ellen and me."

What had that been about? Poole wondered. Bonnie had taken over a plate of macaroons when the Loudermilks had just moved in, had said they seemed nice if not a bit aloof. "Books," she'd said, once back at home. "Lots of books. And the art. My God, they have a lot of art on the walls. None of it matches anything. They have a leather sofa. Dark green." But Loudermilk had not said, "Why don't you and Bonnie come over for a drink." Or even, "Why don't you and your wife," or just "you guys," come over for a drink. Was that an accident? Or did Loudermilk have something else in mind? Poole tried to imagine a scenario with him and Mrs. Loudermilk in bed while Kit watched television downstairs. Or watched *them*, more likely. Was that the thrill? Poole shook his head. No thanks, he thought. But he saw himself kissing Ellen Loudermilk's tattoo, her slim, tanned legs rubbing together in pleasure, her wild hair flayed on the pillow.

He saw Kit Loudermilk crawling toward them on all fours, a gold chain dragging across silk sheets.

"Jesus," Poole said. "Jesus Christ." He walked up the driveway to the garage, opened the door. It was barely getting light but he climbed aboard his lawn mower, fired it up. The John Deere always started right away, unlike cheaper models

Reverse Prototype

you saw stalled in lawns all over town. He put the mower in gear and rolled through the door, stopped to engage the blade, turned deftly by the front steps, and started cutting.

John Salter

REDHEAD

Rainy days. Water pooled in the yard, driving birds to the high fringe of grass along the driveway. The gray sky bulged. Graham thought about his revolver three times on Thursday morning. Washing dishes, the Colt in its lethal entirety flashed in his mind. Tying his bootlaces before going out to check the mail, he saw the long, cool barrel. Watching CNN, he felt the sharp checkering of the walnut grip against his palm. He was afraid to go into the bedroom because the revolver was in the bedroom closet. How long was the bridge between involuntary thought and involuntary action, anyway? He thought of the insane slapping their own heads. This was too creepy to deal with so he pulled on his jacket and fled the house.

Grady's Café was swollen with people escaping the gloom. There were no booths available. Graham sat at the counter next to a sugar beet farmer in a brand new John Deere cap. The farmer leaned back to regard Graham with the unabashed interest of a big landowner, accustomed to endless leafy fields the color of money. Graham nodded and feigned great interest in the menu but when the waitress paused before his place he ordered only coffee. He wanted to smoke but the ashtray between him and the farmer was clean and he didn't want to offend so he added cream and sugar to his coffee for something to do. He wished he'd bought a paper. He felt the farmer awaiting contact and hoped he'd be ignored but in the end he turned to the farmer and spoke first, a preemptive strike. "Some weather."

"For a duck."

"I suppose it doesn't help you guys very much."

"It's early yet."

"They're saying a week just like this."

"They're saying."

He was rescued when another farmer came into the place and made a show of stomping his boots in the entryway, an easy habit in Minnesota where snow remained on the ground six months out of the year. The second farmer sat next to the first and the two enjoyed some gossip about a third farmer. Graham went ahead and lighted a Marlboro and drank his coffee fast and when the waitress returned he kept it black although the coffee was less black than the color of a brand new penny. At home he drank muddy coffee from morning until night. His wife thought he was crazy. "You twitch and jerk all night long from drinking coffee and smoking. You should just quit." Emily had no bad habits. He imagined her lungs as pink, sweet fruit; his own as mildewed burlap sacks.

He drove into Fargo. The streets were like Beirut, torn up and blocked from rain-delayed construction projects. At stoplights people glared at each other. Midwestern congeniality followed the sun. He thought about turning around and going home but the idea didn't take hold. Like the farmers and cement contractors, Graham wasn't working much lately, though his lag had nothing to do with the weather. He taught part-time for a branch of a branch of a college with dubious accreditation and his classes for the term had been cancelled due to weak enrollment. This was the second time it had happened in as many terms. Emily had been encouraging him to find something with more stability. They weren't going broke—Emily held a good job at the Post Office, a career position with good benefits—but there'd been a noticeable degradation in their quality of life. Small luxuries had been dropping from the radar screen like doomed aircraft. HBO had been cancelled. Their twice-weekly dinners out had become sporadic dinners out, and Graham noticed a little sadly that Emily always steered the car toward the cheaper places, Denny's or its many clones and even McDonald's. Graham for his part had gone from his favorite Sumatra beans purchased at coffee shops, to the more common beans from the grocery store, and finally to whatever canned variety was on sale.

"I haven't seen you in what? Three years?"

Graham nodded, trying to place her. She had long red hair, and Graham didn't know that many redheads, but still, she didn't come to mind. He imagined she was a former student. This had happened before. He understood that later on that night, maybe days later, her name would interlock with her face and he'd remember her, where she'd sat in the room, even what she'd written. "Right," he said. "At least."

They were standing near the entryway to the mall. Graham had just come in; she was on her way out carrying a Dayton's bag, did a double take, and he'd stopped. Now she reached out and touched his arm. "Is everything okay?"

"What? Everything's fine. This weather, though."

"I know. Isn't it a bummer?"

"Gloomy," Graham said.

"So what are you up to?"

Graham shrugged. "I had to get out of the house. I was going stir crazy. What about you?"

She held up the bag. "I'm going to a wedding this weekend. None of my old dresses fit anymore."

She didn't look overweight, just a little bouncy. "Well," he said. "That can happen."

She twirled in a clumsy pirouette. "I've lost twenty three pounds."

"That's great," Graham said. "That's an accomplishment, all right."

"Well, we're not all born skinny like you."

"No. That's a fact."

"Listen," she said. "I'm dying for a cup of coffee. I'll buy you one."

"Great."

"Is there a place here? I can't remember."

"Me neither," Graham said. He looked down the corridor but saw only people moving quickly over the tiles like the clouds in *Koyaanisqatsi*. "There's a place by the bookstore about a block from here. I go there sometimes."

"I'll ride with you," she said. "I get all disoriented in Fargo."

He studied her on the way to his pickup. He wanted to think her name was Karen but then he remembered that red-haired Karen had been from Texas, and had a serious accent. Plus Karen had been a stubborn student, trying to turn every essay into an anti-abortion tract, and they'd parted on less than loving terms.

If not Karen, then who? As if reading his thoughts the woman glanced over at Graham and smiled broadly. She was attractive. He always remembered the very attractive students the way he always remembered the very socially awkward, the problematic, the borderline illiterate. Graham pointed at his pickup, huddled like a

Redhead

frightened turtle between two huge SUV's. "The Chevy," he said.

"You'll need an ark before long."

"You're not kidding. They're saying more of the same all week."

"Yuck. This wedding is supposed to have an outdoor reception, too."

Graham unlocked the passenger door and opened it. He went around and climbed in. The windows were heavily fogged from the bad seal. It was an old truck, half the time in need of repairs. "Sorry for the mess."

"That's okay. You should see mine. I think I have the world's biggest collection of empty Diet Coke cans."

Graham started the engine. He turned the fan up full-blast. "It'll be a minute to clear the window."

She reached out and turned the heater off. "I like it this way."

He looked at her. She stared at him through partially slit eyes. "I used to imagine being alone with you."

Graham nodded.

"I always kind of thought you did, too."

His tongue felt thick, a wooden drawer swollen from the humidity. He nodded again, gripped the steering wheel.

She slid over to him, pressed her hand against his thigh. Her nails were bright orange. "This is like fate, running into you."

He watched her fingers walking up his leg. Her thumb brushed the bulge in his jeans. Her lips met his and a thousand hot embers landed on his spine. He untucked her blouse and ran his hand up to her breasts and felt small, hard nipples through lace. The windows darkened even more. Her jeans came off. She pushed him down. He pressed his face between her breasts while she climbed aboard. He listened to the rain pounding against the roof. She came quickly with a low moan and he followed and after there was only a sense of dampness permeating everything from the marrow to the sky.

He drove home, a little faster than normal, a little panicked. When a semi passed him the pickup was enveloped in a cloud of spray and it occurred to Graham that he could ride in the cloud forever if he stayed right behind the semi. But he let off the gas and could see again. He wasn't sure what he felt. Everything had happened so quickly. Less an affair than an assault? He lighted a cigarette and rolled down the window a few inches and drove

John Salter

east letting fat drops glance against his face.

At home, Graham showered, went heavy on the soap although he was a little sad to drive away her scent. He threw the evidence into the washing machine and went back upstairs and brewed a pot of coffee. When she'd left the pickup she'd said, *that was one hell of a cup of coffee* and he'd laughed for quite possibly the first time in weeks. He'd held her pale hand briefly and then she was gone. "Stay in touch," she'd said. "I've got the same number."

"Me too," he'd said.

He went to his study and found his old vinyl covered grade books, saved reluctantly as a hedge against litigation. You never knew these days what students would pull. He sat at the dining room table in the dim light and went back to the beginning of his short career and studied the names. Olson. Jenson. Schmidt. Olsen. They meant nothing to him. A few struck him as names he should remember but the reasons evaded him. He flipped to the most recent terms and worked backward. He couldn't find her. One or two names struck him as possibilities but when the accompanying faces emerged in his memory they weren't hers.

"So what did you do today?" Emily asked, stripping off her work clothes in the bathroom. "I tried calling but you were gone."

"I went to town."

"For?"

Graham scooped up her sweatshirt and pants and dropped them down the laundry chute. "I went to Job Service."

"And?"

"I didn't find anything."

"You tried, though. That's the main thing. Good for you."

"Things will work out," Graham said, his stock comment.

The phone rang after dinner. Graham moved to answer it but Emily was in the kitchen and snatched the receiver from the wall, laughing at his clumsy dive. "Hello?"

Graham watched her brow furrow. "This is she."

He went to the sliding glass door overlooking the deck and cracked the door. The smell of rain forced its way in.

"Really?" she was saying.

He shook a cigarette from the pack on the table and lighted it, blowing the smoke through the gap and into the night.

Redhead

"That is unbelievable," Emily said. He turned to look at her. She screwed up her face. Graham raised his eyebrows.

"I'm not interested in that," she said.

She hung up.

"Who was it?"

"An unbelievable long distance offer."

Close to midnight, lightning struck nearby. Thunder vibrated the window.

"Are you awake?" Emily asked, quietly.

"I'm awake."

"I've been awake forever," she said.

"Me, too."

She turned to face him. Her heavy, unfettered breasts pressed against his arm. In the lightning flashes he saw the pattern of the blinds on her broad, brown hip. Her hand rested on his stomach. "You're gaining weight," she said.

"A little."

"So do you want to work some off?"

"I don't know."

Her hand moved lower. He fought arousal but her fingers knew him.

After, he imagined savage, microscopic troops spreading out in her womb, digging in.

"Everything is complicated," he said, to her back.

"What do you mean?"

"People are complicated."

"No, they aren't," she said.

"You don't think so?"

"I don't think so. Everyone wants the same things. How is that complicated?"

"Then it's how they get there," Graham said. "That's where it gets complicated."

She didn't answer.

"You hear me?"

"I'm tired now."

Up very early, Graham made breakfast for his wife, scrambled eggs with cheese, bacon, orange juice. "This is nice," she said, fresh from the shower.

He shrugged. "Trying to keep myself valuable."

John Salter

"At least you still shave and clean up. Valerie was telling me that when her husband was laid off last year he went something like three weeks without taking a shower. All he did was smoke and eat peanuts and buy baseball cards. She came this close to divorcing him."

"I believe it."

She reached out and patted his hand. "So I'll keep you for a little while."

"I won't stop shaving but I am thinking about dying my hair red."

"What?"

Graham smiled. "Sure. Fresh start."

She rolled her eyes.

"I mean, think about it. It would be unique. How many redheads do you know, anyway?"

"More than I want to know."

"What's that supposed to mean?"

Emily chewed a piece of bacon and stared at him. He poured her more juice. "Thank you," she said.

"What about redheads, anyway?"

"Oh, I don't know. If we're talking real, you know, true redheads. I went to school with a girl with red hair. Freckles, the whole bit. Biggest bitch I ever met. Real manipulative."

"What happened to her?"

"Ramona? I don't know. Wait. She married some guy in the Army and moved to North Carolina. Maybe Georgia. I don't know."

"Have I ever met her?"

"I haven't seen her since graduation. Thank God."

Graham reached back and opened the sliding glass door a few inches and lighted a cigarette. "I don't know if I've ever met a redhead."

"You'd remember it. They're always a little different. Cocky or something."

"I had a redheaded student but I don't know if she was a true redhead."

"Only one way to tell, dear."

He felt his face starting to flush. He stood and went to the door and leaned out, let the moist, cool air help return his normal, pallid tone.

"You know what, honey?" Emily asked.

"What?"

Redhead

"I love you but you come up with some weird breakfast talk."

"Maybe I have too much time on my hands. Maybe I'm going crazy."

"No comment," she said.

Saturday. Graham spent the morning in the basement using a floor squeegee to push water, seeping through cracks in the floor, toward the sump hole and the overworked pump. It was maintenance work—the water returned immediately—but he was antsy and didn't mind this sort of pointed pacing.

The ceiling above him creaked with Emily's footsteps as she tidied up the house. They were getting company in the evening, friends of Emily's from the Post Office. Trivial Pursuit was on the agenda, chips and salsa, beer. Emily and Dave would gossip about people at work while Graham and Linda made small talk. The kind of get-together he looked forward to until it drew close, like any trip he took, where his interest was soon replaced by a general sense of dread.

She came to the top of the stairs. "We need booze. You want to go or should I?"

"I'll go," he said. He leaned the Squeegee against the wall and went upstairs.

"Bud is on sale at River Liquors if you want Bud. Otherwise go anywhere you want."

He changed into a clean sweatshirt and went to the door. It wasn't raining very hard but it was misting. He hurried to the pickup and climbed in. He thought it still bore the aroma, however faintly, of the affair. The affair? The incident? "Mistakes were made," he whispered. He laughed. "We had to destroy this village in order to save it."

He drove into Fargo. On a whim he swung by two Lutheran churches. At one of them he saw a man in a tuxedo smoking a cigarette under an overhang. Did he know the redheaded woman? Graham kept driving. He went to River Liquors and bought a case of Budweiser, wine coolers, a pint of butterscotch Schnapps which he opened and sipped from on the way back home.

The Buffalo River was high, near the level of the bridge. "Andrea," he said aloud. "Amy. Amanda." He took a pull on the Schnapps. "Brenda." He paused. He couldn't think of any more B names. He saw a bewildered looking horse in a field. He parked on the shoulder just past the bridge and slid across the seat and rolled down the window. "Carla," he called out to the horse. "Christine. Cindy." The horse regarded him blankly for a few moments, then shook its head wildly. Water sprayed from its mane.

"Delilah," Graham shouted.

The horse turned and trotted away over the muddy ground.

His groin itched and he didn't know if it was normal itching or something else or if it was only his imagination. He thought of the contact, brief but with the terrible force of an Alberta Clipper. Despite the worries he became aroused by the memory. He allowed himself a few terrifying scenarios: the redheaded woman married to a jealous biker. The redheaded woman bearing his first child. The redheaded woman aborting his first child. Finding the redheaded woman at the break table with Emily one of these days when he brought her lunch.

The sky broke on Sunday afternoon. Graham was stretched out on the sofa, watching professional golf. At first there was only diluted brightness spreading across the hardwood floor toward him like spilled oil. Then a shimmering, otherworldly glow. Emily padded in from the bedroom carrying the Wal-Mart ad from the newspaper. "Gas grills are on sale. We should go take a look."

"Sun's coming out," Graham said, nodding at the window.

She turned to look. "Well, it's about frigging time."

Graham pulled on his cap and they went outside. Steam was rising from the blacktop driveway. "The grass will be going wild after this," he said.

Emily bent to press the back of her hand against the lawn. "Soggy."

They climbed into Emily's Mazda. Neighbors were emerging to stand outside, pale and surprised, like Holocaust survivors. Bicycling children materialized on the road as if the rain had dissolved them only temporarily. Out on the highway, Emily turned up the radio and they bopped to Van Morrison. She squeezed his hand. They reached the bridge. Water was receding from the banks of the Buffalo River so quickly, and with so little drama, Graham thought, you wouldn't remember the flooding unless you really wanted to.

Redhead

Noyland with Mother and Child

"Noyland, going west."

These were Noyland's own words, uttered aloud in his car, at a quarter to noon. Noyland liked to caption himself as he went about his life.

Noyland, changing the oil in his Grand Prix.

Noyland, pleasuring his wife while thinking of woman whose face he has never seen.

He pulled into the first rest area west of Fargo. She'd said the first and then two days later he'd wondered if she meant the first coming from Fargo or coming from Jamestown, where she lived. He didn't know if there was more than one. He hadn't been west in years. His cryptic email question had gone unanswered for seven hours until finally he'd received an equally cryptic response: *Go west, young man, to the first oasis on your right. No camels but maybe one-twelfth of a harem.*

His wife, Esther, never talked like that.

Noyland, jogging along the Red River to build endurance.

He parked under a canopy of lush elms and watched people coming and going. The road was flush with travelers unworried about getting caught in a whiteout blizzard. The atmosphere at the rest area was festive. No serial killers lurking by the Pepsi machine. Noyland felt a great burst of enthusiasm, vigor. I do want to live, he thought. I am happy to be alive in the twenty-first century.

Noyland, making an affirmation.

She'd said noon but also that "circumstances" could make her late. Noyland suspected the circumstances were her children. Kyle? Kyra? Kjell? K names for sure but so easy to skim past in the hunt for words that drew his breath away, words like *bored* and *asshole husband* and *together for the kids' sake. Fantasy. Oral sex.*

At a quarter past, Noyland climbed from his car and knelt on the pavement and reached under the car seat for the cowhide belt-pack he'd gotten in Deadwood, South Dakota, on a long-ago trip with Esther. The gold lettering was faded. He set the pack on the hood and unzipped it. Survival goods. Three condoms. Toothbrush and paste. His handgun, a .38 snubnose Colt. He squeezed one of the condoms through the foil. It felt springy. Ready. He tossed the pack into the car and wandered up the neat sidewalk to the Pepsi machine. He fed a dollar into the machine, watched it come back out. He smoothed the dollar on the upright edge of the machine, pulling it back and forth with some real panache, and tried again. Dollar accepted. Noyland took his Pepsi and sat on the edge of a picnic table. He watched a young married couple frolicking in the grass with their Labrador Retriever. The dog ran up to Noyland and bit the toe of his alligator cowboy boot. "Sorry," the wife said, hurrying over.

"That's okay. Nice retriever."

"Thanks. We just got him."

"A dog like that will do fifteen hundred dollars in damage before he's grown. Chewing mostly. And scratching. Not including what he'll ruin with crap and urine."

"Well," the woman said. "That's something to think about." She hoisted the puppy, held it upside down like an infant and went back to her husband. She whispered something to him and they both glanced at Noyland before going back to their car, a tidy Mazda. Illinois plates. Noyland felt bad for making their North Dakota experience a strange one, but he was only speaking the truth. He and Esther had owned a retriever years earlier, a Chocolate Lab, when it became apparent that children were out of the question. They'd never gone for tests, but Noyland believed he was the sterile one, and he was bitter about being an adult sterile male in the age of AIDS when condoms were being thrown at everyone with remotely motile hormones, and not back in the seventies, when men could act like Hugh Hefner as long as they didn't knock anyone up.

Noyland, born too late for the glory days.

Their dog had been hit by a truck hauling sugar beets when Noyland and Esther were riding their tandem Schwinn near the Buffalo River east of town. Noyland still heard the single yelp sometimes, followed by Esther's wail on the seat in front of him. Noyland always provided the power on their excursions and allowed Esther to steer. He was glad he hadn't seen the accident.

Noyland with Mother and Child

They'd never bothered to get another dog.

At one-o'clock Noyland watched a white minivan turtle its way through the parking area and pull up between a Winnebago and his own Pontiac. The woman driving spent considerable time adjusting her big 1980s hair in the rear-view mirror before climbing out. She looked appropriately apprehensive. Noyland knew it was Angelica. He felt relief. He had foreseen a few different scenarios and one of them involved Esther trapping him even though he doubted she had the technical know-how or even a suspicious enough mind to retrieve and decipher his email notes. And he had worried that Angelica's husband might appear, thus the revolver in Noyland's belt pack. The revolver was also his cover. "I'm going shooting," he'd announced that morning to Esther. She had an almost visceral reaction to guns and didn't even bother to ask where he was going to shoot, or when he'd return.

Noyland watched Angelica scanning the rest area. She started toward a gaunt man smoking by the posted map of North Dakota but then a woman emerged from the restroom and joined the man. Angelica turned, spotted Noyland, and strolled by as if on her way to the Pepsi machine. He smiled. "Quite an oasis," he said.

She stopped. "Noyboy?"

Noyland slid off the picnic table. "Finally."

They embraced. "This is weird but not weird," she said.

"I know what you mean." He studied her, soaked up her details like an albino absorbing the sun. Angelica had dark hair streaked with light. Her skin bore evidence of an adolescent plague of acne. She wore a sweater that made her breasts pointy cones. Esther's breasts were fuller but tired, like the skin under her chin. Angelica stood on slender legs. And wore a skirt, Noyland saw, happily. Esther, self-conscious about her stout legs and thick ankles, owned only one skirt, had worn it only for a funeral, driving Noyland batty in the church pew to the point that he'd disgraced them both by sneaking his hand between her legs during the eulogy.

"Well," Angelica said.

"I was hoping you'd come," Noyland said. He shook his head.

"You're even more beautiful than I imagined."

"Come on now."

John Salter

"I mean it."

"What did you expect, some kind of Martian?"

Noyland shrugged. "You never know. What about you?"

She stared blankly at him. "What about me?"

He stepped back and spread his hands. "Am I what you expected?"

"About."

"I mean, I'm no Bob Redford."

"You're fine."

"Well."

"Listen," she said. "I can't stay very long."

Noyland, on the brink.

They walked toward the van. Noyland fell back a few feet and studied her healthy rear. In one of her emails she'd written that her husband was preoccupied with her bottom and for some time had refused to make love anymore unless she allowed him entry in "the back door," something that frightened her. Noyland had been quick to point out that he shared her revulsion and that normal intercourse with an interested partner would never bore him. This exchange had come about after several notes that hinted at a failing marriage. Noyland had exaggerated his own frustrations. In truth he was just bored, but boredom was such a cliché he'd alluded to a violent wife with an addiction to her asthma inhaler. Now they were together near Interstate 94, a white humming ribbon, getting ready to commit adultery.

She opened the sliding van door and they climbed inside. The middle seat had been removed. "It's easy," she explained. "You flip these little thingamajigs and it pops right out. You can haul a lot more this way. I'm going to Sam's Club later."

"That makes sense."

They sat on the bench seat. "Lots of leg room this way," Noyland said.

She laughed. "Oh. I brought something." She climbed up over the seat and rummaged around. Noyland started to touch the backs of her knees but pulled his hand away. She turned around with a bottle. "

"Champagne."

"Classy."

"It's nonalcoholic."

"That's okay."

Noyland with Mother and Child

"I figured since we're both driving and all."

"I'm already drunk on your beauty."

She shoved him playfully. "Get out."

Noyland unscrewed the lid.

"I forgot to bring glasses," she said.

Noyland took a long pull from the bottle. It tasted like warm grape juice. He handed her the bottle. She had a sip.

"I feel like we've been talking for years."

"Me, too," Noyland said.

They kissed. Her mouth was harder than Esther's. For some reason Noyland imagined kissing a coconut. He slid his hand between her knees and she locked it there, halfway to home. "Not yet," she said. But she didn't release his hand, either. Her thighs were cool. His fingers started to cramp. She parted her legs and lifted her rear from the seat and pulled her skirt up, pushed her panties down. Noyland kissed her knees. She moaned and pulled Noyland's head toward her womanhood.

Noyland, going in deep.

The baby cried at the exact moment Angelica was squirming in either an actual or very convincing fake orgasm. At the sound, Noyland increased his efforts, thinking the rising screech and Angelica's twisting torso were a result of his expertise in this, a gift Esther accepted only rarely. Then Noyland glanced up and saw the fuzzy top of an infant's head as Angelica lifted the baby from the cargo area behind the seat. Noyland backed away from Angelica and wiped his mouth on his University of North Dakota Fighting Sioux sweatshirt. He felt a hair on the roof of his mouth but thought it would be impolite to attempt removal. "You brought a baby," he said, not knowing what else to say.

"Kyle. He just turned eight months."

"Good looking baby."

Angelica jostled the now silent baby on her bare knee. "My neighbor was going to watch him but she got called into work. I couldn't take him to my mother-in-law's because she'd be suspicious."

"That's okay," Noyland whispered.

She thrust the baby at Noyland. "Hold him?"

Noyland joined them on the seat. He took the baby, tried to hold him in the crook of his arm the way he'd held his newborn nephew in the hospital a decade earlier. But Kyle was too big and

John Salter

fought the strange position. So Noyland wound up bouncing the baby on his knee, the way Angelica had, while she pulled up her panties and straightened her skirt. She looked at her watch. "I suppose," she said.

"I better be going, too," Noyland said.

"I'll email you later."

"Ditto," Noyland said. The baby smiled at him, a serene little Buddha. Noyland laughed and pretended to snatch Kyle's button nose.

"What a cutie."

"He's my sweet one. My other two got all the rotten genes."

Noyland kissed the baby's forehead. He sniffed the baby's hair. "He's got that new baby smell and everything."

"I love that smell."

Noyland poked the baby's belly. "Gotta love this baby," he said.

Noyland, with mother and child.

Back in Fargo, Noyland went to Grady's Café and drank a cup of coffee while reading the *Fargo Forum*. He'd already read the paper, early that morning, while having coffee with Esther on the deck. But Noyland thought people alone in restaurants drinking coffee without doing anything else looked a little screwy, so he read the paper again.

"More coffee?"

He looked up at the waitress, a girl in her early twenties. Becky talked with her mouth almost shut to hide a pierced tongue. The pierced tongue was the latest in what seemed to Noyland to be a string of increasingly dramatic acts of rebellion. Long hair became short hair became purple hair. Orange lipstick and nail polish became black lipstick and nail polish. Six earrings running up her left ear became a diamond stud on her nose became the pierced tongue. Becky alluded—not to Noyland but he'd overheard the allusion—to more exotic piercing locations in the future. Sometimes, Noyland wondered about her parents, imagining them as frail, worried people, with hands rubbed raw from fretting about their daughter. Now he wondered if her parents had done something to set her on this course. Some gaffe that banked her in the wrong direction, like a cue ball wobbling toward an inevitable scratch. He thought of Kyle, wedged behind the seat, listening to his mother receiving cunnilingus from a man, not his father.

"Can I ask you something?"

"Shoot," Becky said. She had a flat and not very attractive face but had, a time or two, occupied the stage in Noyland's fantasies.

"Do you remember being a baby?"

"Do I remember being a baby?"

"Yes."

She craned her head to look at the newspaper as if the catalyst for the question might be in an article or advertisement.

"That's a really interesting question. Why do you ask?"

"I can't remember being a baby," Noyland said. "But I'm wondering if someone your age can."

She cocked her head and closed her eyes. "I can remember falling off my trike. But I wouldn't have been a baby. I would have been a toddler. Oh—I think I can remember my great grandmother. She died when I was a baby."

"What do you remember about her?"

"Itching."

"Itching?"

Becky smiled. "Yes. I didn't remember it until right this second but I remember feeling itchy after she held me. Scratchy. It's hard to explain."

Noyland, probing the human brain.

Esther was reading on the sofa when Noyland went home. She went to the library every Saturday morning and carted home mysteries. What she liked about mysteries was the never-ending supply, she often said. There were zillions of ways to murder someone; in fact, she argued, there were more ways to kill people all the time. So the mystery novels would keep coming.

She closed her book when Noyland came in. "I was getting worried. What if you accidentally shot yourself in the head and nobody found you?"

"I went for a cup of coffee."

Esther puckered her lips and closed her eyes. Noyland bent to kiss her. If she was alone for too long she tended to get a little needy. Her warm, puffy lips felt like home. Her eyes flung open. "What's that smell?"

"Smell?"

"On you. I smell something."

John Salter

"I don't."

She beckoned. He backed away.

"Come here."

"I don't want to be smelled."

"What were you doing?"

"I told you. I went shooting and then I had a cup of coffee."

"Then why are you acting like this?"

"Like what?"

She picked up her book. "Whatever."

Noyland, dealing with his stubborn wife. He foresaw days of cold silence, an empty bed. He went into the kitchen. He breathed into his palm and sniffed the trapped air. Coffee. He went back to the living room. "I don't know what you're talking about," he said. He sat next to Esther. "I was thinking we should go out to eat."

"Fine."

"Where should we go?"

"There it is. I smell it again."

Noyland sighed.

She leaned close and sniffed audibly. "You know what? You smell like a *baby.*"

"A baby?"

"Yes. That's it. You smell like a baby."

"That's impossible."

"I smell a baby. That baby smell."

"I don't."

"Were you holding a baby today?"

"Where would I be holding a baby?"

She glared at him.

At dinner Noyland ordered a burger and made a point of eating the onions and not prodding them off the meat like he usually did. Esther eyed him sullenly. It didn't help that a young couple with infant twins sat behind her. The twins looked unhealthy, underfed, compared to Kyle. He regretted not making up a story about the baby. It would have been so easy to just say he ran into an acquaintance and held their baby for a moment. He'd panicked, though, thinking she smelled another woman on him. Even now he thought he could still taste Angelica, the way alcohol couldn't be permanently covered with a breath mint.

"What would you say to getting another dog?"

Esther stared blankly at him. "A dog?"

Noyland with Mother and Child

"Sure."

"We've been through this."

"I'm thinking a little dog this time. Like a little wiener dog, or a little schnauzer. He could ride in the bike basket."

"The last thing we need is another dog."

"What about a cat, then?"

"You hate cats."

"I could live with a cat."

She put her fork down. "What are you trying to accomplish, Noyland?"

"I want you to be happy."

"I want to go home now."

He woke for his customary middle of the night urination, a new feature of his late-thirties. Esther wasn't in the bed. Hard to tell, he thought, going into the bathroom. Sometimes if he snored too much or thrashed in his sleep, she bailed for the sofa. But if she was angry she left, too. He shut the lid to mute the flush and crept into the living room. Esther was wrapped tightly in her afghan. He went into the sewing room slash office and turned on his computer. He checked his email for a message from Angelica but there was nothing in the folder but a Viagra joke from his brother-in-law. He sensed that he wouldn't be hearing from Angelica again. The presence of the baby had been too weird, stripping away a layer of anonymity. That she'd even bring a baby to meet a stranger concerned him. He wasn't a freak but he could have been a freak and involving a baby was irresponsible to say the least. He remembered Kyle's spastic, gummy smile and grinned broadly himself, almost involuntarily. He went back to bed and pulled the covers over his head. In time, he thought he could smell the baby himself, very faintly, in the warm, still air around his body.

Noyland, smiling for unknown reasons.

Noyland, for unknown reasons, weeping.

John Salter

Big Ranch

Although free to walk around, Anna Lee never left the island of brittle grass on which the cabin, barn, and bunkhouse sat. There was no point. She had been told more than once that a high steel fence surrounded the ranch, a fence wired to a series of iron rods planted up and down the spine of the Sierras. Hank had flipped open the encyclopedia and shown her just how often lightning struck the earth. Sometimes, the sky demonstrated this to her, and while she'd never seen the fence, not even through Hank's spotting scope, during storms she thought she could hear the metal sizzling.

And even without the electricity to worry about, there were cougars beyond the fence, and bears. The ranch was too remote for television signals but there was a big-screen Sony and VCR and a stack of movies that grew every time Hank and his guests came up to hunt and fish. One of the movies was about a huge grizzly that wandered into a summer camp and devoured everyone except a beautiful blind girl and a counselor with bulging muscles not unlike Hank's. Bullets could not stop the grizzly, as an unfortunate game warden discovered, but the counselor and the blind girl, both excellent swimmers, lured it into the river, into the rapids. The grizzly went over a waterfall and died, although Hank said it would probably turn up again, in a sequel. Bears similar to the one in the movie had been spotted, Hank added, trying to burrow under the fence, and they had a preference for eating Indian girls.

So the safest place to be was in her quarters, in the old bunkhouse, with its heavy oak door and massive deadbolt for which only Hank had a key. The windows were small, up near the ceiling, designed more for venting the body heat of sleeping cowboys than adoring the view of the pasture, the dark screen of trees, the mountain peaks. To see out, Anna Lee had to stand on her rocking chair, on two encyclopedias, with her fingers curled over the sill for balance. Still, she was happy she didn't live in an airy canvas tent, like those in the movie, vulnerable to sharp claws and teeth.

She stood in the doorway and watched Hank drive in, slowly, his tanned arm dangling from the window to bisect the gold King Lumber Security star painted on the door. The star was lined with scratches from driving on narrow, brush-crowded dirt roads. For a while, Hank had been driving a new pickup every couple years, but this one, a battered Chevrolet with a deep crease in the rear bumper, had been around so long the other trucks appeared in Anna Lee's memory as simple smears of color, like blurred faces from her past. The one time she'd asked when he was getting a new truck, after it wouldn't start one chilly November morning, Hank had just laughed. "Not until they find a way to make big timber grow faster."

He honked and waved. She waved back. She had known he was coming soon. She was down to only two Diner's Delight microwave dinners, both macaroni and cheese, her least favorite, but Hank had never allowed her to run out of food. She was on a schedule: dinner, her big orange vitamin, the little white baby pill, and an hour with her exercise videotape before bathing and going to bed. If she skipped even part of the routine, Hank often warned her, everything would go to hell. The vitamin wouldn't work without food, and without the exercise, the food would just sit in a pile in her stomach. She would die.

She started for the driveway, to help unload the pickup. Hank always came up a day or two before bringing guests, to stock the cabin and check things out. Sometimes he brought tools and lumber, and made repairs. Once in awhile, though not often, he showed up very late at night, smelling of smoke and beer, and slept with her in the bunkhouse. On these strange nights she did not get much rest because Hank twitched, swore, jerked, and cried, snoring loudly through it all.

Without speaking, they carried in cases of Budweiser and Corona, frozen steaks, mesquite chicken breasts, Pepsi and coffee, milk and eggs. Toilet paper. For her, more microwave dinners. Her freshly laundered nightgown and underwear in a plastic bag. Kotex.

They sat on lawn chairs, on the porch. Hank smoked, watched a hawk wheeling in the sky far above the pasture. He turned his fingers into a pistol and shot it. He looked at her. "Anybody come

John Salter

around, last couple of weeks?"

"Yes," she said. "A Jehovah's Witness." She recalled the dusty green sedan, the smiling, dark-skinned man ambling up the driveway clutching a brochure.

Hank laughed. "That's ambition." He squinted at her. "Anything you need to tell me about that?"

From the bunkhouse, she'd watched the Jehovah knock on the cabin door, then peek in the windows through cupped hands before coming toward the bunkhouse. Because of the angle she'd lost sight of him, but with her ear pressed against the heavy door heard him whistling, heard the scuffing of his shoes on the steps. The Jehovah had rattled the latch. Later, back at her window, she'd seen him going to his car, pausing to urinate on the dry grass with his head tilted back, his eyes closed.

"No," she said. "He wasn't here very long."

"Good."

"Was he a test?"

"Doesn't matter," Hank said, reaching down to squash his cigarette butt under his cowboy boot heel.

"You never tell me. I wish I knew when it was a test."

"No you don't. You get that grill cleaned up like I told you? All that grease?"

"Yes," she said. "We need more propane, I think. The tank was easy to lift."

Hank nodded. "Be three of us coming up tomorrow. Me plus two."

"Is Grant coming?"

Hank stared at her. His eyes were watery blue, the corners webbed with lines. She had told him once, after they watched *Cool Hand Luke*, that he looked like Paul Newman, only older. "Well, he's Jewish," Hank had said, but seemed pleased. Now he grinned. "You liked that boy, didn't you? Grant."

She nodded. Grant had not fucked her. He'd asked only for a pencil, and on the sheet-rock wall above her bureau, drew a picture of her while she sat on the floor with her legs straight out and her hands planted behind her. From time to time, he'd walked over to rearrange her long hair, or tilt her head. She still remembered the feel of his smooth, warm hands under her chin. Grant had a wife, he'd said, and a baby named Paige. He didn't like working for King Lumber. He wanted to teach high school art, something he'd gone to college for. Anna Lee had broken a rule, then, one of Hank's big rules: *Never talk about yourself, even if they ask*. She'd told Grant about an art project in the seventh grade, a vase she made for her aunty on the pottery wheel, one of only a few pieces in the class to survive the kiln firing. While carefully penciling in her eyes, Grant asked where she'd gone to school and Anna Lee froze up, suddenly afraid it might be one of Hank's tests. But Grant hadn't pressed the matter. "Have you ever seen the ocean?" he'd asked. She hadn't, except in movies. So Grant drew the Pacific Ocean on the wall, too, along with a sailboat and gulls. She was worried Hank would make her wash it off, but so far, he hadn't.

"Well," Hank said. "Grant won't be coming back."

"He won't?"

"He's not with the company any more. Be me and Pink and another guy."

"Is he teaching high school?" she asked.

Hank shrugged, stood abruptly. "Come inside. I need to be getting back pretty soon."

After, she stood naked before him, hands down at her sides. Hank reached out from the edge of the bed and pinched her hip. "What is this shit?"

She looked down. Her hip bore his fingerprints, a trail of fading white circles on her brown skin.

"You been doing your tape?"

"Every night," she said.

"Getting too easy for you?"

"No. I burn."

"You bored with the Fonda? They got new ones now. All kinds."

"I like Jane."

"Well." Hank motioned with his finger for her to turn around. "Someday I'll enlighten you about Hanoi Jane. Tighten up now."

She tensed her muscles. Felt his rough hands on her rear, poking, squeezing. He turned her sideways, leaned back, sighted along her belly. Lifted her breasts, let them flop down. He sighed. "Anna Lee, you're getting old. No doubt about it."

"I am?"

"You are." He pushed himself up from the mattress, slapped his own belly, mounding over the waistband of his boxers. "We all are."

John Salter

She laughed and squeezed his biceps. It was hard, the skin over his Navy tattoo still taut although the color had faded even in the ten years she'd known him. Hank regarded her fingers. The room was very quiet; the low afternoon sun striped them both in shadows from the trees in the yard beyond the big picture window. He covered her hand with his own. Their eyes met and he looked away. "Try to fix those nails up before tomorrow night."

On cool evenings, whenever she made a fire in the tiny sheepherder's stove in the bunkhouse, Anna Lee remembered, saw her uncle Raymond whirling her aunt Aletha in a sweeping circle, throwing her against the orange-hot stove in their company house on Indian Hill. Saw her aunty flopping on the metal, arching her back, her lips pulled back in a smile that wasn't a smile, saw Raymond stomping his wife with his knobby logging boots, hitting the floor half the time because he was sloppy drunk, shaking the house, vibrating the windows, knocking Anna Lee's vase from the shelf, sending ceramic puppies toppling over the edge. She remembered reaching out from her hiding place under the coffee table to rescue them, her uncle grabbing for her thin arm. Saw herself slipping past him, out the door, almost running into Hank's pickup as he churned up the muddy road from the mill. Hank pulling her into the cab, saying *down, down, down.* Hank taking her away, up to the ranch, while she stayed on the floor like he'd told her. "Good girl," he'd said. "Good girl."

She sprayed a cloud of Elizabeth Taylor White Diamonds into the air and walked briskly through it, something she'd seen done in a movie. She put on her black kimono and perched on the edge of the bed, and waited. She knew it could be ten minutes or it could be an hour. Or not at all. Sometimes, Hank said, men weren't interested. People were complicated, he said. That would explain the men who sometimes broke into tears afterward, or the men who kept their eyes closed the whole time, or men like Grant who drew pictures on the wall.

She picked up an encyclopedia but put it down right away. She studied her freshly painted fingernails. China Rose, the color was called. She looked around the room. She wished that she smoked, so she would have something to do while Hank and Pink and the other man, who she hadn't seen yet, sat on the front porch drinking and talking about hunting, lumber, Japan,

Sacramento, Washington. It was always the same talk. The other man was new so he would be first. Pink would be tomorrow night. She was glad. She didn't like Pink. Pink was mean, called her names the whole time.

The door opened. A fat man wearing a floppy camouflage hat with a snap-brim came inside. He dropped his duffel bag. Blinked. Took off his glasses, wiped his sweaty face with his sleeve. Turned to look back outside. Hank and Pink were laughing, the sound fading out as they walked back to the cabin.

"My, my," the fat man said. He took a long drink from his Corona. "Hank said the bunkhouse wasn't such a bad place to sleep."

Anna Lee smiled, patted the bed.

Under mounds of flab, through the grunting, the stink of nervous sweat and alcohol, Anna Lee found a shaft of fresh air drafting through an ancient nail hole in the wall. She thought of *Bridge on the River Kwai*, William Holden breathing through a reed. Or was it another movie? She couldn't remember. The fat man was having trouble. This had happened more times with more men than she could remember and she had learned ways to help, *rope tricks*, Hank called them, but the fat man pushed her away. He lowered his heavy feet to the floor and leaned forward as if his belly hurt. Anna Lee turned on the bedside lamp. Sometimes it helped if they could see her.

The fat man kept his eyes on his knees. "What are you looking at?" he hissed.

Another rule: *Never give up*. She smiled, crawled over to him, ran her fingernails along his thigh. Nothing. He grabbed his Corona from the nightstand and stood, walked over to the wall. The fat man regarded Grant's picture, licked his thumb, rubbed at one of the gulls until it was a black smudge, a dead raven. "Piece of shit," he said. "Where did Hank find you, anyway?"

Anna Lee sprang from the bed, came up behind him, gripped his puffy, pale shoulders. She pressed her cheek against his back. "Want a massage? Loosen you up."

He spun around, slapped her ear. She hit the floor. He moved fast for someone his size. He grabbed her hair, jerked her up to the bed, pushed her face into the pillow. She felt the rim of his Corona bottle, icy wet, running down her back. She shivered. The fat man was panting. His entire weight seemed to be on his

John Salter

left forearm, against the back of her neck. The bottle went lower. The fat man grunted, screwed it into her roughly. Lightning bolts flashed in her skull. A rule was being broken, though not by her. She thought of Jane Fonda and pushed up mightily. The forearm slipped and the fat man began to roll. He clawed wildly at the air and toppled from the bed. His head struck the corner of the sheepherder's stove with a sound like an axe blade burying itself in green wood. His great, fleshy body shook wildly. The Corona bottle dropped from Anna Lee and rolled across the floor.

"Well, this is a problem," Hank said. He sat on her rocking chair, smoking. He studied the tip of his Salem. "Cover him up, will you?"

It hurt to move, but she dragged her sheet over the fat man. Her blood was on the sheet.

"This motherfucker is a state legislator," Hank said. "Was a state legislator."

"What's that?"

"A big time mucky-muck. Get dressed now."

"A boss?"

"What? Yes. Big boss."

Pink had come in right behind Hank. Now he was out in the yard, vomiting. Anna Lee pulled on her panties, her jeans. She found her King Lumber sweatshirt but Hank shook his head. "Not that shirt. Wear a plain one."

She put on one of Hank's old white t-shirts. He nodded. They listened for a few moments to Pink retching, swearing, coughing. Hank looked at her and rolled his eyes.

"Is Pink a boss, too?" she asked.

Hank groaned, stood. "Right now, everybody is my boss. The whole goddamn world is Hank's boss, right about now." He prodded the fat man's belly with the toe of his cowboy boot. "Son of a bitch. A beer bottle. What gets into people, anyhow?"

Pink appeared in the doorway. The skin that had given him his nickname was gray now, the color of the weathered antlers mounted above the bunkhouse door. Pink did not look at Anna Lee or the fat man. He glared at Hank. "We're fucked, you know that?"

Hank squatted by the Corona bottle. It looked smaller than it had felt, Anna Lee thought. On the floor, in a pool of beer, it seemed innocent. Incapable of harming anyone. She watched

Big Ranch

Hank pick up the bottle delicately, with two fingers, and examine it briefly before placing it on the fat man, in a deep crevice in the sheet. "Just relax," he said quietly.

For a moment Anna Lee thought he was talking to the fat man, but then Pink spoke up. "Relax? Are you kidding me?"

"Go inside, have a drink. I'll take care of this."

"You fucking yokel," Pink said. He wiped a string of vomit from his cheek. "You have any idea what's going to happen when this gets out?"

Hank straightened up. His knees popped. "So this drunk bastard took a spill and banged his head. So what?"

"You really believe it's that simple."

"He fell down," Hank said. "End of story."

"You're forgetting about something, Flynn. Someone."

"There is no someone." Hank glanced at her. "Someone doesn't exist. Hasn't for ten years."

Pink's bald head went from gray to pink to red. He jabbed a finger at Hank. "You won't exist. I won't exist. King fucking Lumber won't exist if your little Paiute whore ever gets tired of country life."

Anna Lee gazed down at the fat man. "I didn't mean for it to happen."

The men ignored her. Pink threw up his hands. "You swore that when the time came, you'd deal with things."

"I will. I'll move her for awhile"

"No."

"You're in this too," Hank said. "It shouldn't all be on me."

"It is on you. You brought her up here. You have the gold star on your truck. Your hands have never been that clean, anyway. What's a little more dirt?"

Hank lit another cigarette, glared at Pink. Pink glared back. A long time passed. Anna Lee stared at the wall, at herself, pretty on the beach, smiling at the ocean.

"I'll drive," Pink said.

It was cool in the yard. The sky was clear, the ranch illuminated by stars, the full moon. Hank gripped her by the arm and they followed Pink to the cabin. "When we get back," Pink was saying, "we'll clean everything up and haul that fat fucker down the hill, find a hospital."

"Whatever," Hank said. His fingers tightened on her arm. He

yanked her close and for a few steps they walked as one. She smelled his breath, smoky, sweet from brandy. When Pink opened the screen door and went inside, Hank's lips brushed her ear. "Run," he whispered. "Go and keep going."

She ran. Headed for the trees beyond the pasture. She heard Hank cursing, heard the screen door screech open, slam shut. Her rear end was on fire but she bit her lip and kept going. She reached the pasture, tripped on the ragged fringe of weeds, rolled on the ground. She looked back as she scrambled to her feet. Pink was in the yard already, with his deer rifle, striding toward her.

Close to the jungle-thick trees, she remembered the fence, ten feet high, the current strong enough at times, according to Hank, that birds landing on it burst into flames. She slowed down. Her stomach hurt. Everything hurt. She stopped, turned around. Pink was almost across the pasture. Farther back, Hank was walking in tight circles, hands on his hips, looking up at the sky. Bears, she thought. A grizzly could outrun a horse in a quarter mile stretch. She tried to step into the trees but her legs wouldn't allow it. She did not want to be eaten alive. She closed her eyes, listened to the footsteps getting closer. Maybe, she thought, brightening a little, maybe it was only a test.

Healing Paths

In Boulder, on Pearl Street, a very pale girl with dirty hair thrust a blue velvet pillow at Smoky when he paused by her wagon to get his bearings. "Smell it," she said.

"Say again?" Smoky asked.

"Go ahead. Take a whiff."

Smoky closed his eyes and inhaled. The pillow smelled vaguely like marijuana. He opened his eyes. "What's in here?"

"Sweetgrass. Sage. Plus some batting, but it's a hundred percent biodegradable."

Smoky nodded. He looked past the girl, at the sign on her wagon. *Spirit Pillows*, it said. The sign was decorated with crudely drawn southwestern symbols: lizards and howling coyotes, Kokopele tooting on what looked more like a joint than a flute.

It's a great scent," the girl said. "It's basic. Plus it's real tactile." She reached for his left hand and pressed the pillow against it. "See?"

"Nice," Smoky said. Her hands were cold. She could not have been more than twenty, he decided. She had eyes like a llama's, big and far apart. He looked down at the pillow. It was lumpy, misshapen, like something a slow child might fashion in school. The sadness of the effort made his eyes tear up. It did not take very much lately to make him cry. He let go of the pillow and turned away quickly.

"Hey," the girl said. "Hey!"

Smoky glanced back. The pillow was on the ground.

"Asshole," she said.

He drove up to the National Center for Atmospheric Research, in the hills west of Boulder. He'd seen it from the outdoor café where he'd gone for lunch. He'd thought the squat, brown building might be a mosque, and had imagined becoming a Muslim for awhile, cleansing himself in the high desert under strong guidance. His trip to Rocky Mountain National Park, to backpack and sketch wildflowers, had left him feeling grimy and lonely and nowhere nearer to being optimistic than when he'd left his home in northern California with a carload of new and expensive camping gear. Structure, he'd decided, picking at his Greek olive salad. Structure might be the ticket.

But the waitress had said, "That's not a mosque, whatever that is. It's encar. It's hella cool. It doesn't cost anything to get in."

He didn't go inside. He cruised past row after row of cars and minivans, dodging families of tourists, and parked at the edge of the lot. He sat on the hood of his Thunderbird and lighted a cigarette and looked down at Boulder. The smoke, coupled with the altitude, made him so dizzy he had to lean back on the windshield to keep from toppling over. He had quit smoking when his girlfriend was pregnant, and although Helena later miscarried, he hadn't thought about taking it up again until walking out of the mountains. Exhausted, trying to motivate himself to keep going, he had created a list of things to do when back in civilization, the way he'd read some prisoners of war did in their bamboo cages to keep from going insane. *Steak dinner with a baked potato and extra butter and sour cream. Ice cold beer. Cigarettes, strong ones. A long, water-wasting shower. Cable television.*

He'd planned five days in the park but cut the trip short after two, finding the mountains dry and colorless, the wildflowers uninspiring as roadside dandelions. He was lonely and wanted to call home, but didn't want Helena to know he'd quit so early. He imagined her rolling her eyes, bringing up the aborted effort in the future whenever he complained of feeling desolate. He drew on his cigarette and exhaled, watched the smoke twitch away schizophrenically in a sharp breeze. A day more and he'd call, he decided. That would be acceptable to Helena.

The trip had been her idea. Actually, Bob Good, her boss at County Mental Health, had been the one to suggest it when they got together to play softball against County Social Services, but Smoky was pretty sure Helena had asked Bob to encourage him. She'd been concerned ever since he mentioned, over dinner, that he felt an odd and forceful urge to cut his own throat with the Chicago Cutlery steak knife he was using on a ginger pork chop. The impulse had passed immediately but the comment left Helena visibly alarmed. "That's not normal."

"Sure it is," he'd said.

Helena had stared for a long time at the steak knife as if it might jump from the edge of Smoky's plate and disfigure her. "No, it's definitely not normal."

"You mean you've never felt like crossing the center line and hitting an oncoming logging truck? Or walking out on the tundra until you're exhausted, and going to sleep?" The latter was something he'd just seen in a television documentary on Eskimos. It sounded painless, dignified.

"Never," she'd said.

Now he opened his eyes and stared at the sky. He wondered if Helena was shacking up with Bob Good while he was away, if the advice to get closer to the sun, to break his routine, had only been part of a plot. He tried to picture Helena squirming under Bob's tan, yoga-enhanced body, but the image did not take root long enough to spark either rage or excitement. He felt tired, suddenly, and decided to go back to his room for a nap.

On the winding road to town, Smoky almost hit a man in a wheelchair. The man was going awfully fast for such a steep grade, Smoky thought, and at that moment the wheelchair swerved, almost tipped, crossed in front of the car, and rolled into the roadbank. The man, a stout Indian wearing a black Stetson, was almost ejected when the chair stopped abruptly.

Smoky stopped the car and jumped out. The man was trying to back up but his wheels could not gain traction in the loose, red dirt. "Are you okay?" Smoky asked.

The man nodded. He looked embarrassed. "Shit. Too much speed, I guess." He had a southern accent. Coming from an Indian, it took Smoky aback, the way he was always a bit surprised to hear Black people with British accents speaking on television.

"You want some help?"

"Hell, yes. I'm a lot less stupid than I am proud, partner."

Smoky tried pulling the chair out by the handles but the angle made it impossible and left him out of breath. The man laughed. "Be careful now or you'll break your back, too. Then we'll really be in trouble."

They wound up turning the chair around to face the road and with his shoulder, Smoky was able to free it. The man popped a wheelie, let the chair bounce hard. Sand shook loose from the frame. "Appreciate it," he said.

"Do you want a ride?"

The man looked down the road. "That might be okay. I'm flat

worn out from getting up here this morning."

His name was Curly, he said, after Smoky had helped him into the front seat, folded the chair, and shoved it into the trunk. "Half Okie and half Choctaw." He squinted at Smoky. "You're something, aren't you?"

"Excuse me?"

"Indian. Indian and something else."

Smoky nodded. Nobody, save for Helena, had ever seen it in him. "A fourth Penobscot."

Curly nodded. He stabbed a finger at the pack of cigarettes on the dash. "You mind, cousin?"

"Go ahead," Smoky said. He allowed a quick glance at himself in the rear-view mirror. His time at high altitude had given him a ruddiness that did, he decided, reveal more of his heritage than usual.

Curly lighted the cigarette with a silver Zippo that appeared and disappeared magically in his big, gnarled hand. He regarded the burning tip. "Penobscot. Penobscot. Where are they from again? Montana, isn't it?"

"Maine," Smoky said.

"That's right. Maine. I knew it was an *m* state. Shit, you're a long way from home."

"I live in California now," Smoky said, reaching for his own cigarette. When he poked it into his mouth Curly's lighter materialized again. "Actually, I've never been to Maine."

"It's still your home. Home is always where your people are," Curly said.

Smoky nodded, stopped at the bottom of the hill. "Which way?"

"Well. Shit." Curly shrugged. "That's a damn good question. Maybe straight. Go straight and I'll figure it out." He turned to look at Smoky. "If you don't mind, little brother."

They ended up at a coffee shop, not a cappuccino place like Smoky would have preferred, but an old-fashioned café populated with sunburned, harsh-looking locals. Smoky was aware that all eyes were on him and Curly, especially when they wrestled the chair through the narrow doorway, a task not accomplished without a fair amount of unabashed grunting by Curly. But he seemed not to notice the scrutiny, or care about it if he did. He rendered his coffee a roux of sugar and cream and smoked cigarettes from Smoky's pack. "You're wondering how I came to be in this thing," he said.

"Not really," Smoky said. It was a lie. He had already decided Curly was too young to have been in Vietnam, and too awkward with the chair to have been born in need of it. That left a number of dark possibilities.

"I'm a bull rider," Curly said. "Oklahoma state champion in eighty and again in eighty-four. Take a look." He wheeled back from the table and pulled up his heavy belly with both hands to reveal a glittering gold rodeo buckle.

"Nice," Smoky said, leaning forward to look. The buckle was crowded with engraved numbers and words, though he didn't want to get close enough to actually read them.

"I was on my way, brother. Had my eye on the nationals."

"I believe it."

"You bet." Curly raised his mug in a sort of half toast. "On my way."

"I couldn't do that," Smoky said. "Ride a bull. They're so massive. I get nervous around horses, even."

Curly shook his head. "I never had a problem with it. I never got hurt bad on a bull. Not a once." He slapped the wheelchair. "This here is from getting throwed out the bed of a pickup down around Ponca City."

Smoky gazed into his coffee cup and nodded.

Curly laughed. "Don't even feel bad, brother. This isn't forever."

"That's good."

"I went to a healer."

"Here in Boulder?" Smoky recalled seeing no end of alternative medicine listings in one of the Boulder brochures he'd picked up at his motel. He was halfway thinking of going to see a phrenologist himself.

"The healer's back home, back in Oklahoma. He's the real deal."

"I see."

"I'm on a quest, man. I got things I have to do. All kinds of weird shit. Like the first stage. Then I go back to the healer."

"Interesting," Smoky said.

Curly lighted another cigarette, leaned back in his chair. "That's why I went up to that old weather place on the hill. One of the things on my list, the healer told me, he said to touch a whirlwind."

"A whirlwind? Like a tornado?"

"Exactly. A tornado."

"That's got to be hard to do," Smoky said.

"Shit, yes, it's hard to do. You try it sometime. Sit around all day listening to the police scanner, watching the Weather Channel, getting your mother to drive you around in storms. I never did see a whirlwind, let alone touch one."

Smoky shook his head. The disbelief on his face was genuine. He was wondering what kind of sadist would have a paraplegic out on such a dangerous snipe hunt.

Curly glanced around, then lowered his voice. "The spirits. They're on my side. Came out here to this weather place to see if they could help me out, look on their computers and all that, help me find a whirlwind."

"Sounds logical."

Curly smiled. "I didn't even need their computers. They got this little tornado cooked up in there for people to look at. A miniature whirlwind." He held up his hand. "Scratch that off my list. I reached in and touched it. I touched it for a damn long time."

"That's good," Smoky said. I'm glad for you."

"Think it'll count?"

"I don't see why not."

"Me too." Curly stared at his hand. "It's a real whirlwind, it's just in a box is all."

Back in the car, on the way downtown, Curly reached out abruptly and gripped Smoky's thigh. "I only told you all that on account of you're people. You know what I mean, brother?"

"I think so."

"Shit, I know you do." He let go of Smoky's leg. "You got some muscle there. You run?"

"I walk," Smoky said. The answer immediately struck him as insensitive. "I mean, I just got finished backpacking in the mountains."

"My woman, Wind, she's into all that. She's a mountain girl. I'm going with her just as soon as I get rid of this son of a bitch."

"Sounds good," Smoky said.

"She's downtown right now, down at the street mall. She's an artist. She's not people, like us, but she's okay."

Healing Paths

"What kind of art?"

"Pillows," Curly said. "Sews these pretty little pillows. Got bad dreams and all that, nightmares, these pillows will chase them right out. Guaranteed."

Smoky sat in his motel room with the sliver view of the mountains. *Jeopardy*, one of his favorite programs, was on the television but he was having a hard time paying attention. He was worried he'd insulted Curly when dropping him off at the Pearl Street Mall. Earlier, in the café, Smoky had been convinced that Curly would ask for money, so in the restroom, he'd separated his bills, putting the bulk of his cash in his left pocket and a single ten dollar bill in his right. Years of being a soft touch for pan handlers and friends had taught him this trick. He could simply draw out the lone bill and hand it over, claiming it was all he had, allowing him to retain most of his money while looking like a good guy. It seemed a slick solution, although Helena frequently pointed out that he could just as easily learn to say no.

But Curly had not asked for money, had not even hinted. He'd only wanted Smoky to meet his girlfriend, Wind, the same pillow maker, Smoky assumed, who'd called him an asshole. Smoky had gotten out of the introduction by feigning the need to make an important phone call, and had immediately tried to give the ten dollar bill to Curly, who'd looked genuinely confused. "What's this for?"

"Just a little something to help you out."

"Hell, Smoky, I don't need money. I wish it was just money I needed."

Curly had pocketed the ten, anyway. "Wind wouldn't mind you buying one of her pillows," he'd said. "It might give her a boost." Then he'd asked Smoky where he was staying. "We'll bring your pillow by later."

They'd been blocking traffic and a line of cars had built up behind the Thunderbird, the drivers too polite to honk, given the wheelchair, but nonetheless impatiently edging closer. Smoky had been hard-pressed to come up with a good lie so he'd told Curly he was staying at the Starlight Inn, room fourteen.

Now Smoky puffed away at one of the few cigarettes remaining in what had been an almost full package before Curly got to it. He regretted giving up his location. The wise thing would be to pack up and drive back to California, he decided. Surprise Helena. Or take a different route, check out the scenery. He flipped open his atlas and studied the possibilities. Tracing his route to Colorado, he realized he'd driven by Salt Lake without noticing the water. He wondered how he could have missed something so immense. But even camping in the mountains, waking to urinate at dawn, the misty splendor had excited him less than if he'd discovered a drowning moth in the toilet back home. He stared blankly at the map. Nothing interested him. He looked out the window. The sky seemed brittle. He stretched out on the bed and began to weep. Lately it seemed the only honest response to the weight of his life.

It was dark out and Smoky was dozing when Wind arrived. He lurched to the door and flung it open to find her standing there, looking a bit sullen, holding a pillow out like a ring bearer at a wedding. "Are you Smoky?" she asked.

Smoky nodded, relieved that she did not seem to recall him from earlier in the day. "You must be Wind. Come on in." He made room for her and leaned from the door to scan the parking lot. "Where's Curly?"

"Asleep," she said. She stood rigidly at the foot of the bed, gazing at the tacky seascape mounted above the headboard. "Curly always goes to bed by nine. He gets up early to pray."

"Right." Smoky swung the door back and forth, slowly, not sure whether it would be appropriate to shut it. Wind spun around to face him then.

"Why were you crying today?"

"Say again?"

"At the street mall. You started crying."

Smoky felt his face reddening. "I don't know. I just do, sometimes."

"Koyaanisqatsi," she said, nodding sharply.

"Excuse me?"

"Are you out of balance?"

"Maybe," Smoky said. He took the pillow from her and set it carefully on the television. He felt mildly annoyed. He didn't like having his head shrunk, by anyone. "So how long have you known Curly?"

"In this life? Two years."

"Well."

"Listen," she said. "Think it would be okay if I used your shower? We're camping and it's been awhile."

Smoky looked at the pillow. It was not the same one from that afternoon. This one was smaller, grimy around the edges, as if handled quite a bit. "I guess so," he said.

He was very conscious of time as he listened to the water running through the flimsy bathroom door. He tried to watch CNN but could not help imagining Curly waking, looking at his watch. Conclusions could be jumped to, especially when she returned fresh from a shower. And who knew what sort of virility issues Curly was dealing with? Smoky aimed the remote at the television, hoping to find a sitcom, something cheerful, distracting. He tried to remember if he'd left anything valuable in the bathroom.

The water stopped. The door opened, and Wind emerged from the steam, naked. She did not act self-conscious at all, but anyone named *Wind*, Smoky decided, probably wouldn't have normal interior censors regulating her behavior. Smoky blushed, feigned great interest in the television. Wind walked over to the table and sat down across from him. "I rinsed out my tee-shirt," she said. "That's why I took so long in there."

"That's fine," Smoky said.

She lighted one of his cigarettes. "I don't like to waste water. Water has a soul like everything else and it doesn't like being taken for granted."

"That makes sense," Smoky said.

"I love water, period. I wouldn't mind drowning. I wouldn't fight it."

Smoky shook his head. "I would. I'd panic."

"I know you would. I can tell it's not your element."

"Probably not," Smoky said. He felt acutely aware of his movements, as he did when forced to dance. Thankfully, the tabletop cut off much of her body but her round, pink breasts were like interrogation lights glaring at him. "So how do you like Boulder?" he asked. He tried to meet her eyes while the words came out but his rhythm was off, and he imagined the result looked like a poorly dubbed foreign film.

"I love Boulder. Everyone here has the right attitude. It reminds me a little of Jackson Hole, which reminds me a little of Santa Fe."

"What does Santa Fe remind you of?"

"Nothing. It's the source, dude. It's where it all begins. We're

John Salter

going to live down there after Curly gets healed."

Smoky nodded. "He's pretty serious about that, isn't he?"

"He was on the healing path when I met him and that's been two years, like I said. But he's almost done now."

"He told me about the tornado. The whirlwind."

"Well, he must trust you, then, because he won't talk to just anyone about that shit. It's real heavy."

"It sounds heavy."

"There's a lot of negative energy out there. That's why he doesn't talk about it." She rolled her head, cracked her neck on both sides. "Curly doesn't need any negativity, that's for sure."

"I try to keep an open mind about things," Smoky said. He was finding it a bit easier to look at her. Inside, scrubbed clean, away from the harsh sunlight and the carnival atmosphere of Pearl Street, she looked soft, almost pretty. Less jaded, anyway. "Back home," he said, "back in California, there's a man who had his shingles cured with some tea an old Maidu woman gave him. He drank it every day and his shingles disappeared. It blew away the doctors."

"This is bigger than tea," she said. She stood abruptly and walked over to the door, still open a crack, and pushed it shut. Smoky snuck a glance at her rear end but its youthfulness made him feel old, even at thirty, and a bit deprived. She returned to the table and stubbed out her cigarette, squinting at the window, either at her own reflection or the tiny lights flickering along the mountains. Smoky studied her image in the glass. Her skin looked ghostly. He imagined she was getting ready to leave. He felt both relieved and disappointed. Here I am, he thought, in Boulder, Colorado, with a naked girl in my room. He smiled, wondering what Bob Good would say. He was wondering what Helena would say, when Wind abruptly grabbed his hand and jerked him like a bullwhip to the bed.

He woke at daybreak in a panic that shrunk only slightly when he realized Wind was already gone. He wanted to blame the night on a dream but the bed smelled heavily of sweetgrass. Wind had put the spirit pillow to some creative use, he could remember that much, but now it sat on the nightstand, innocent as a pincushion.

He was carrying his backpack to the car when he heard his name. He turned around. Wind was on the sidewalk, holding a tall foam coffee cup which she handed to him without expression. "Leaving?" she asked.

Smoky nodded. "Yes. Well, I think it's about time I moved on. Time to get home." He took a sip of the coffee. It burned his tongue.

Wind crossed her arms. "You seem in a hurry."

"I thought you were gone. I thought you went back to where you're camping."

She looked into the trunk at the heap of clothes, freeze-dried food, maps. "Where's the pillow?"

"It's in the backpack," Smoky said. It was a lie. The pillow was in the trash, under the contents of the ashtray.

"Well, will you give me a ride?"

Smoky stalled by drinking more coffee although it was still hot enough to make his eyes bulge. He preferred his coffee lukewarm. "Are you sure that's such a good idea?"

"What do you mean?"

"You know. After, you know, being with me. All night, all that."

She rolled her eyes. "You mean the sex?"

"Right."

"Don't worry about it."

Driving east on a two-lane, listening to Wind singing along to the country station, Smoky fought his uneasiness by promising himself that within an hour, tops, he'd be turned around and on his way to California. An interesting experience, he thought, this little trip to Colorado. He would tell Helena, and Bob Good, too, that although he didn't necessarily feel completely renewed, just getting away had been helpful. Souvenirs, he thought. He would have to stop and pick up some souvenirs. A magnet for the refrigerator, maybe a Colorado sweatshirt for Helena to wear while she worked in the garden in the early evening.

"Not too much farther," Wind said.

Smoky glanced at the odometer. They'd gone nearly seven miles already. Had she walked that far? "Quite a ways from town," he said.

Wind shrugged and turned up the radio. Smoky looked at her. He found it hard to believe that she'd spent the night with him. Actually, he'd been more surprised than aroused and even in the midst of her stormy thrashing, he'd felt detached from his own body, not entirely there, almost anxious for it to be over. It was similar to when, up in the mountains, he'd spotted a golden eagle in a tree and wanted it to fly away because he'd felt more obligated to stand still and watch than truly interested.

Halfway down a rolling hill, Wind leaned forward and said, "Turn in at this next cattle guard."

Smoky had not seen a sign advertising a campground. Of course, he thought, they probably couldn't afford one, probably relied on the good will of landowners, perhaps rodeo people. Smoky imagined the champion buckle and wheelchair could go pretty far in that respect. He slowed the car and pulled in, stopping as soon as the tires cleared the cattle guard. He surveyed the rutted dirt road ahead. There was nothing but low hills and scrubby brush in sight, no houses, not even a mobile home. "How far in is it?"

"Not that far," she said. "Just around the bend."

"Maybe I could let you off here."

She shook her head. "Curly wants to see you."

"Well."

"Please," she said. "He's counting on you." There was a pleading quality to her voice that broke Smoky's heart. Her llama eyes were large, unblinking, her thin lips pressed together as it to stifle a sob. He fell in love with her and reached out to squeeze her thigh. She pushed his hand away. "Drive," she said.

Around the bend, Curly waited, a bright Pendleton blanket across his lap. There was no evidence of a camp, no fire, no ashes, not even a sleeping bag. Smoky thought this was strange but filed it away to contemplate later, more concerned with remaining nonchalant as he walked with Wind toward the wheelchair.

"Morning, morning, brother," Curly said. His teeth flashed brightly in the shade of his cowboy hat.

"Good morning," Smoky said. He looked around. "Pretty spot."

Curly looked at Wind, raised his eyebrows. She nodded gravely and quickly stepped away from Smoky, drawing a huge clasp knife from her back pocket. Smoky raised his hands. "What is this? What's going on?"

Curly smiled. "The last thing on my list, brother." He folded the blanket back, revealing a long-barreled revolver which he lifted and pointed vaguely at Smoky.

Healing Paths

"The car?" Smoky asked. "My money?" His voice was high, whiny. He cleared his throat, backed up a few feet. "Take what you want."

"We're not robbing you," Wind said.

Curly laughed. "We'll probably use your T-Bird, though. It's a sweet little ride."

"What's this all about?'

"I told you, brother. The last thing after touching a whirlwind. It's on the list. Got to eat the heart of my strongest enemy."

"Don't blame Curly," Wind said. She opened the knife. It clicked audibly. "He didn't make up the list."

"I'm not your enemy, though," Smoky said. "I'm your friend. I'm part Indian. I'm people, remember?"

Curly jerked the chair around until his side faced Smoky. "You are my enemy. You fucked my old lady."

"That's right," Wind said, glaring at Smoky. "I didn't like it, though, baby. I told you I wouldn't."

"You knew?" Smoky asked. He glanced around for cover. The car was a good fifty yards back. "I'm not your enemy if you wanted me to do it."

Curly nodded. "Yes, you are."

"Technically speaking," Wind said.

"It won't count."

"All I know is I got to eat the heart of my strongest enemy," Curly said. "You're it, brother." He rested his elbow on the armrest and aimed the revolver.

"I'm not strong," Smoky said.

"Sure you are. Hiking all over. Mountain climbing."

"He's strong," Wind said. "I should know."

Curly cocked the revolver. "I don't have time to wait for a better enemy to come along, Smoky. I don't get back on the bulls pretty soon, I'll be too old to compete, see?"

A bullet whipped by Smoky's ear. He heard it as one would hear a bee. Wind was moving toward him with the knife, striding purposefully through the brush.

Smoky ran for the car. Another bullet grazed his sleeve. He screamed. His voice, shrill and piercing, shattered the dry air. Color returned to the mountains. The ground felt alive, moist under his feet. The earth sang to him.

John Salter

THE NEW TERRITORY

Her orange running shorts, glowing like a low harvest moon in the field next to the truck stop, caught Raymond's eye. She limped, bent under her duffle bag. Stopped every few yards to adjust her load, looking around each time as if to refresh her bearings before trudging on through the long grass.

Raymond figured she was homeless. He was used to seeing drifters at the truck stops where he always fueled his Mercedes. He'd been told the heavy truck traffic ensured fresh diesel, which would prolong the life of the car, a gift to himself to celebrate the addition of North Dakota and eastern Montana to his territory. The car was not brand new but the retired professor he'd bought it from had kept it up, and Raymond intended to follow suit.

As the woman drew closer, Raymond could see she was not very old. Not more than twenty-five, thirty. An Indian woman. She paused at the edge of the parking lot to scrape her muddy shoes against the asphalt. She was not bad-looking, Raymond thought. She walked to the building and propped her bag against the wall. It fell over. When she reached to lift it, Raymond admired her long legs, a nice pair of stems as they'd say back at the office. She glanced around and went inside.

Raymond pulled a Squeegee across the windshield with long, sure strokes. He hated a dirty windshield. A single bug smear in his line of sight could drive him nearly insane over the course of a hundred miles and it was not uncommon for him to pull over, even in traffic, to scrub the glass with the cleaner and rag he kept in the trunk. Summertime was the worst.

He looked over the hood at the Indian woman's bag. He imagined it contained everything she owned in the world. He shook his head. Crazy, he thought, living that way. Wandering, begging. Sleeping under bridges. At least, he decided, the Indian woman was dressed for the season. She couldn't be all crazy. Other drifters always seemed to wrap themselves in winter coats and hats, even in the dog days of August. Their faces were always covered with a thick sheen of sweat. Raymond had seen a few up close when they'd approached him for change or cigarettes. The sight had turned his stomach. This was before he'd learned to stare through the drifters as if they were only windows to something more interesting.

The Indian woman emerged shortly with a bottle of Pepsi. She stood by the duffel and took a long drink, eyes closed. Raymond studied her. He liked her long cheekbones, her reddish-brown hair, her aquiline nose. He thought her pretty face helped offset her wrinkled, outdated clothes and droopy breasts. She opened her eyes. She looked at him for a moment before hoisting her duffel and striking out across the parking lot. She walked right by Raymond as he was replacing the squeegee. He could see she was clean. Her skin looked clear and cool. Her wake smelled vaguely of perfume and freshly cut grass. Raymond was surprised at the hoarseness of his own voice as the words rose from his chest. "Which way are you going?"

She froze. Turned around only partway. Her profile spoke. "West."

"Me, too," Raymond said. "You look like you could use a lift."

She shrugged. "I guess."

Raymond dug for his key. He stabbed it into the trunk lock. The lid sprang open. "Throw your bag in. I'll be out in a second."

The cashier whose face had been looming in the window seemed a bit smug when Raymond slapped his American Express card onto the counter. It reminded him of the reaction he sometimes got when he bought *Penthouse*. Raymond glared at the cashier until her face reddened and her fingers trembled over the credit card machine. He looked past her and saw the Indian woman waiting by the car. Waiting for him. He leaned over the counter to check out the adult magazines in the rack. They suddenly seemed amateurish.

By the time they hit the interstate, she was asleep or pretending to be asleep. She leaned against the window, the Pepsi wedged between her knees. Raymond didn't mind. He didn't particularly feel like talking. He set the cruise control and leaned back in the seat. He liked driving. Nobody else had wanted Dakota-Montana when it opened up. It was the distance, the solitude. But Raymond had gone straight to Mr. Henry and offered to take the route in addition to his territory in eastern Minnesota. It was

John Salter

the kind of thing, he'd told his wife, Candace, that Mr. Henry would remember when one of the walking dead vice-presidents moved on and a slot opened up.

He wondered what tribe the woman belonged to. She did not resemble the Indians at the casino he and Candace occasionally drove to. The casino girls were generally chubby. Short. This woman, he decided, resembled the Indians he'd seen in Montana a few summers before when he'd gone out to fish at the lodge owned by the company. He'd flown to Missoula and rented a car for the drive north. On the way, on the Flathead reservation, he'd stopped at a dingy store to buy a package of Dutch Masters cigars. The girls in the store had been thin and taller, like the woman in his car.

He drummed the steering wheel with his fingers. He'd done something foolish in Montana. He'd lighted one of the Dutch Masters but it was so stale he'd thrown it from the car half-smoked. Only after it slipped from his fingers had he realized it might easily start a fire in the dry grass crowding the road. In the airport, he'd read about a man who'd been fined nearly a half million dollars after a major forest fire had been traced to sparks from his chainsaw. Raymond had imagined fire spreading across the plains, overtaking the little town where he'd bought the cigars. He'd panicked. Heart racing, he'd driven too fast for the hills and curves, and even after reaching the lodge, he'd been jumpy. On the way back to Missoula he'd taken a long, convoluted route to avoid the area entirely.

He looked at her again. Her bare brown thighs jiggled in response to the road. He reached over and lowered his hand until it was inches from her skin. He thought he could feel her heat. He wondered what she'd do if he touched her. If he slipped his hand between her legs and left it there. Probably nothing, he decided. He doubted if she'd be surprised. How could she be?

He pulled his hand away. He decided to let her sleep. She wasn't going anywhere.

She woke near Jamestown when a rare curve jostled her head against the window. She stretched and looked out at the road. It was getting dark fast. She toyed with her Pepsi, removing and replacing the cap without taking a drink.

"So," Raymond asked. "You have a name?"

"Christine," she said.

The New Territory

"Christine? I'm Raymond."

She nodded. "I thought you were that guy."

"Excuse me?"

"At the gas station. I thought you were that guy."

"What guy?"

"From the movies. I can't think of his name. He always plays a good guy."

Raymond glanced at himself in the rear-view. "Is that right? From the movies?"

"You look like him. I thought you were him."

"Help me out. What movies?"

She bit her lip. "I can't think of any right now. But he always plays a good guy."

"Really? You like him, this movie star?"

She ran her fingers across the glossy dashboard woodwork. "He would drive a car like this. A fancy car like this."

"You like it? You like my car?"

"It's smooth," she said.

"Beats walking, doesn't it?"

She nodded. Raymond shook a Kool from the package on the dash. He held it out to her. "Cigarette?"

"No thanks."

Raymond shrugged, lighted the cigarette. "You don't like menthols?"

"Don't smoke."

"Really? I thought all Indians smoked."

"No," she said. She turned abruptly to face the door. She opened the window a crack.

Raymond smoked his cigarette. He couldn't believe her, getting sullen like that. Ungrateful, he thought. Ought to pull over, give her the boot right there, miles from town. The nerve.

But the slipstream from her window carried with it a trace of her perfume and he became aroused. "Hey, listen," he said. "I was going on some bad information, that's all."

She remained silent.

"I'll put it out if it bothers you."

"That's okay," she said.

"So you're going west. Where west?"

"Nevada."

"Really? Vegas or Reno?"

"Winnemucca."

John Salter

"Winnemucca?" Raymond shook his head. "Never heard of it."

"There's not much to hear of."

"Are there casinos out there? I went to Vegas a few years ago. I did okay. But it was hotter than hell."

"There's a few casinos."

"So are you going to work out there? In a casino?"

"Family," she said. "I got family there."

Raymond opened his window and threw his cigarette butt out. He watched in the rear-view as it showered sparks on the road. They passed a sign for a rest stop. He thought it might be the last one for awhile. He couldn't remember. He slowed down. He imagined Christine's long legs wrapped around him, her quiet voice in whispers of ecstasy. He took a deep breath. "I don't know about you," he said. "But I wouldn't mind stretching a little right about now."

They stood by a canopied picnic table along the fence, just beyond the circle of brightness thrown off by the pole lights around the restrooms. They were alone, save for a tractor-trailer parked near the exit. Raymond pictured the driver fast asleep, lulled by the idling engine. He moved closer to Christine, until their shoulders brushed together. She did not move away.

Raymond pressed his hand against her back. He thought she might tighten up. She didn't. She seemed to sag a little. "You're a pretty girl," he said. He glanced around, moved behind her, and slipped his hands under her blouse. He cupped her breasts and pulled her close. Buried his face in her hair. "Very pretty," he whispered. He turned her around and worked her onto the table. He kissed her. Not on the lips. He kissed her cheek, her ear, and after he'd pulled off her blouse, her bare shoulder and throat. She did not respond. He could see her eyes in the starlight. She stared blankly at the sky. He began to feel annoyed. She had not said to stop. He wondered what was wrong with her.

"Listen," he said. "I want you to feel good." He slid her shorts down and ran his hand over her hip. "We could feel good here, together."

"You could hit me," she said.

Her voice surprised him as much as the words did. She had not spoken for a long time. "What did you say?"

"Hit me."

The New Territory

Raymond laughed. "I don't want to hit you. I'm a good guy, remember?"

"Hit me," she said.

Raymond slapped her lightly on the cheek. She smiled.

"Harder."

"Are you nuts?"

"Harder," she said.

Raymond slapped her again. The sound was like a pistol shot. Christine writhed under him. "Again," she said.

He slapped her again, very hard, and she began to move in earnest, pulling him into her almost frantically.

Raymond waited by the car. His hand stung. His palm ached like it did when he caught fastballs pitched by his son, Bryce. Crazy, he thought. Wanting to get cuffed like that.

He checked his watch. He felt damp all over. He had a room waiting for him in Mandan. He wanted to be there. Take a shower, call home if it wasn't too late. Candace would be waiting. Reading in bed or sitting on the couch, watching television. He sniffed his hand. It smelled like Christine's perfume. Cheap perfume. Avon perfume, Candace would say. She knew the difference. She had some class.

He lighted a cigarette and looked up at the restrooms. Christine was taking so long he began to wonder if she'd ditched him. If she'd slipped around the building and taken off on foot. The thought appealed to him. He remembered her bag. She'd want her bag, of course. Or would she? He'd been told that Indians weren't materialistic. The professor he'd bought the car from had refused to sell it to an Indian, a pit boss from the casino. The professor had suffered a stroke and drool had trickled from the corner of his mouth. His wife had sopped at it with a rag. She'd had to help him explain. "It would break Frank's heart to watch his Mercedes deteriorate," she'd said.

Raymond had asked what she meant. "Well," she'd said. "They don't get attached to things. So they don't take care of things like we do."

Raymond wondered if the deal about getting hit was an Indian thing. The restroom door opened then and Christine moved down the sidewalk. She walked slowly. It irritated Raymond. She looked even frumpier than before. When she reached him he could see that her lip was swollen. Her cheek was red. "Look," he said. "I think this is as far as I can take you."

She crossed her arms and nodded.

"I bet that trucker would give you a lift. Otherwise someone else will come along pretty soon."

She nodded again.

"Hey, you're closer to Nevada than you were."

"My things," she said.

"Right." Raymond opened the trunk. He lifted the bag out. He watched as she slung it over her shoulder and walked away. He was surprised when she passed the tractor-trailer, when she kept going out to the highway. Well, he thought, as she plunged into darkness. Let her walk all the way to Nevada. He doubted if she was even going there. It was probably just a story. Who had family in Nevada? He shook his head and got into the car. Her Pepsi was still on the seat. He threw it out the window and started the engine.

She had gone nearly a quarter mile by the time he reached her. He caught her orange shorts in his headlights, her peculiar old woman gait. He slowed down as he passed. He caught a very quick glimpse of her face. He thought it was slick with tears but he couldn't be sure. He stomped on the accelerator and roared away. His heart pounded and he thought of that time he might have set fire to Montana.

SCORPIONS

The idea of Allegra came to Graham after a dream in which he walked the floor of a canyon with a cherubic girl who bounded ahead of him, laughing. The walls of the canyon were smooth and wet; the air, moist and cool. The girl plucked a dead, flattened, nearly translucent scorpion from the sand. When she held it up, proudly, the wind took the scorpion from her tiny fingers and carried it to Graham. The scorpion pricked his neck, near his shoulder. Warmth flowed through his body, warmth that transcended the dream; when he woke, he was smiling, giddy. The first thing that popped into his head was the name, Allegra.

Graham told his sister about the dream. Cassandra was a reluctant clairvoyant. She had predicted the fire that killed her husband, Roy, and Sharon, the woman with whom he was having an affair. Although she had not foretold the specifics, Cassandra had experienced a vision while making stir-fry pepper steak, Roy's favorite meal. Staring through a veil of tears at the green peppers and onions dancing in hot oil in the wok, she'd glimpsed two figures: Roy, and a woman she hadn't recognized. Cassandra had watched them writhing in agony for a few moments before dumping a handful of sliced beef over their forms. Later, at the table, she'd said to her husband, "Don't go out tonight," but Roy had anyway, and before morning he'd been reduced, along with Sharon and everything in her trailer near Niagara, North Dakota, to ashes.

Now Cassandra considered the dream. "Well, I don't know. It sounds like heroin."

"Say again?"

"That feeling, from the scorpion. That warmth. It sounds like heroin."

"How would you know?"

"Roy described it to me. He said he he'd tried it in Vietnam. He tried everything. Hashish, opium, cocaine. It wouldn't surprise me if he'd gone to prostitutes."

"Well," Graham said. "It was nice. If that's what heroin is like, I can see why people get addicted."

They were on the screened porch, watching rain sweep down from ragged-edged clouds to the west. The storm was moving their way. Lately nothing excited Cassandra as much as a storm. On calm days, she rocked hypnotically on her worn ottoman, staring into the middle distance, but during storms she brightened, reading close enough to the window that her favorite novels were warped from rain.

She lighted a cigarette and closed her eyes. "I don't know what the dream means. Maybe Allegra is your daughter."

"What daughter?"

"That girl in California. Michelle. Didn't she tell you she was pregnant?"

"She did. But later she said she'd gotten an abortion. She said, 'I can't kill you but I can kill part of you.'"

"What a horrible thing to say."

"Well, she was young."

"Roy used to say things like that. Terrible things."

"I think it was just talk, anyway," Graham said. He didn't want Roy to come up. If Roy came up, he'd be there all day. "I don't think she was even pregnant to begin with. And if she was, I doubt if the kid was mine. Did I ever tell you about the bruise?"

"I don't think so."

"We were, well, making love, I guess is the polite thing to call it. Right around the time we split up. Maybe right after. Anyway, I found this big old hickey on her inner thigh. I mean way up there. It looked like a tattoo of a rose."

"A rose?"

"Life size. That's how big this hickey was. I asked her what the deal was. You know what she said?"

"I never thought to check Roy for hickeys."

"Listen. You know what she said?"

"What did she say?"

"She said it was a bruise."

"A bruise? Was it?"

"No. You're not listening. I said it was a hickey."

"What did you say when she said it was a bruise?"

"Well, I asked her how she got a bruise right there."

"What did she say?"

Graham laughed. He was glad he could laugh about it. "She

said she couldn't remember. She got mad at me for asking. But I mean, if you had a big purple bruise on your thigh, that close, that close to home, wouldn't you remember how you got it?"

Cassandra shrugged.

"I mean, wouldn't you? Come on."

She scooted her ottoman closer to the window. "Probably. Unless I was really drunk or something."

He stared at the clouds. The possibility, though very likely, had never occurred to Graham. It changed things, shifted them, and he didn't like it.

The rain started, preceded by a brisk wind that smelled absolutely of summer. Graham watched Cassandra watching the rain. He carried a burden and was reminded of the burden at times like this. Roy had confessed the affair to him in a drunken, teary monologue nine months before the fire. "Cassandra is crazy," Roy had sobbed. They'd been at Graham's apartment near the university. Roy had come over with beer and tools to help Graham tune up his pickup before Graham left for what was supposedly going to be a new life in California. "I don't know how to deal with her most of the time."

"Hell, she's always been different. Don't tell me you didn't know that when you married her."

"Not this crazy. Not this bad."

"Well."

"With Sharon it's bad, but it feels normal. It feels like a normal thing. I mean, Sharon doesn't start crying for no reason half the time. Last Tuesday I came home and Cassandra was on the floor, all curled up like she had appendicitis or something. Shit. I thought she was hurt but when I asked her what was wrong you know what she said? Guess what she said."

"I can't imagine," Graham had said.

"Dolphins."

"Dolphins?"

"Just dolphins. Nothing else. How do you, what, what do you say to that?"

"Beats me."

"How do you respond to dolphins?"

"That's a good question."

"I mean, I love her. All the way. I just need things to feel normal once in awhile is all. Sharon gives me that."

Graham had done nothing with the knowledge. But

John Salter

sometimes, in his room upstairs, listening to the ottoman springs squeaking, racing the sound of Cassandra's television up the heating duct, he wondered if he might have been able to change the course of events. Threaten Roy, maybe tell Cassandra what was going on. She'd known intuitively but perhaps some outside verification might have boosted her into taking some action. Confronting Roy. Seeing a shrink, maybe.

She looked like a child, he thought. No, not a child, but a painting of a child. A weird child, like in a Balthus painting. A real child would grow bored of looking at rain, of reading the same trashy novels again and again, would want to get up and do something. He started for the door.

"Where are you going?"

"Work."

"Already?"

"I have extra shit to do. We're getting ready for inventory."

"Didn't you just have inventory?"

"We came up short. We're doing it again."

"Will you bring me some cigs?"

"Yes," he said.

Graham got to work almost forty-five minutes early. He parked behind the store, by the dumpster, and cracked the window to vent his cigarette smoke. With the wipers off, the rain soon rendered his view of the university an opaque mish-mash of dim light. He turned on the radio but music seemed intrusive so he turned it low, then off completely. Allegra, he thought. He counted months. If he did have a daughter, she'd be almost three years old. He tried to imagine her, conjured up a smaller version of Michelle; hair so black it was almost blue, like a raven's feathers. Fierce Maidu and Italian eyes. The child would be strong-willed, intelligent, pretty. He wondered what they'd say about him. That he'd died? That he'd run off? Or the truth: that he'd only been around for a few months before family problems took him away, that things with Michelle had basically ended before they really started? That nobody ever bothered to tell him about his child?

The driving rain and accompanying threat of tornadoes kept customers away all night. Graham sent Jimmy Blake home early, at six-thirty instead of nine, and sat in the office smoking cigarettes and doodling on the desk pad calendar. He was Assistant Manager

Scorpions

of Quade's Pit Stop, a fact that still confounded him. When he'd come back from California, he'd gotten the convenience store job purely as a stopgap measure, intending to help Cassandra adjust to life without Roy, then head out to Montana or Idaho. Anywhere with mountains, really. He'd been assured he could return to his job in California helping perform archaeological surveys of proposed timber sale sites, a job that sounded more interesting than it actually was. He'd been putting his archaeology degree to good use examining old beer can dumps in the forest. But it could have been a full-blown Indiana Jones whip-swinging position and he still wouldn't have wanted to be back in the Sierras, near Michelle again. Things with her had gotten messy. There had not been the clean break there should have been. The night she moved out, there'd been some drinking, some mutual shoving around, a wild enough scene to bring the law to his little apartment over the Copper Top Tavern. Even after that, he'd still seen her occasionally; she'd appeared more than once at his door and he'd let her in each time, the memory of her brown, demanding body easily trumping the awareness that she'd betrayed him. That she was too young, nineteen to his twenty-six. That she was trouble. Her mother, Louise, had tried to keep Graham in the web, dropping hints that Michelle was coming to her senses.

"She'll outgrow this before long. She's young, be patient. Let her get it out of her system. She'll need you soon."

"I've got my dignity, Louise."

"You'll both need to get your shit together real soon."

Noon and the sky was clear. Humidity made Cassandra's blouse cling to her so that she looked even more frail than usual. They were out in the yard, picking up garbage from the boulevard, scraps of paper, pop bottles, bits of cellophane, all of which Graham had stealthily planted the night before in a sort of Easter bunny ritual. Yard work was the only way he could get her out of the house lately.

"Will you go to the library for me?" Cassandra asked. She held the trash she'd collected against her belly.

"How about if I take you to the library?"

"I don't want to go."

"It might be good for you."

"What's that supposed to mean?"

"I'm just saying maybe you should get out of the house for

John Salter

awhile. Clean up and put on some different clothes, something summery. Wear some shorts."

Her mouth quivered. She dropped the garbage. "Why are you doing this to me?"

"Get off it," he said, but she was already scurrying up the concrete steps.

He shook his head and bent to pick up the mess, packing it into a black plastic bag. He carried the bag out to the alley and dropped it into the garbage can. There was still water in the can from the rain. It stunk. He was dressed for work and didn't want to risk fouling his clothes, but didn't want to leave the water to draw flies, either. He went to the garage and found the heavy ice chipper he used on the steps in winter, and threw it like a spear at the base of the can. It dented the bottom but punctured the steel. The putrid water streamed out. He felt better from the act.

Cassandra was watching from the kitchen window, smoking, her face contorted and ghostly. Graham couldn't bear it. He went inside. "I'll get your books for you."

"Just forget it."

"I don't mind. Make a list."

"Just get me some Tony Hillermans. Get the oldest and then the next two after that."

"You're reading them in order?"

"I always do," she said.

At work, while Jimmy waited on customers, Graham spread a map of the western United States on the counter. He pulled a yellow highlighter from the shelf, tore it open, and carefully traced a route through North Dakota, Montana, down through Idaho, into Nevada, out to California. It was the reverse of the route he'd taken to get home but no details of mileage or landscape had stuck with him. He'd been wired, on amphetamines, preoccupied with the news of Roy's death. The trip, completed in one shot, had left him sick for days.

Jimmy hovered behind him. "Going somewhere?"

"Jimmy Blake. Master of the obvious."

Jimmy took a bow. "Thank you, thank you." He started to say more but two college girls came in and his attention predictably shifted.

Graham laughed. He liked Jimmy. Almost a year earlier, in an attempt to shake up Cassandra's routine and maybe even spark

Scorpions

a romance, Graham had invited Jimmy over to the house for dinner. Cassandra had refused to cook, had flitted around the kitchen like a bug while Graham hurriedly prepared breaded walleye and baked potatoes. "Why do I have to eat with you? He's your friend, not mine."

"Maybe he can be your friend, too."

"I doubt it. What could I possibly have in common with him?"

"Who knows? What did you have in common with Roy?"

The comment had been like a wind gust, blowing Cassandra to the wall, where she'd occupied herself with picking at flecks of pancake batter, hurled at Graham in an earlier conflict. "Look," Graham had said, talking fast, afraid she'd unravel even more. "Jimmy is in the Air Force. He's traveled all over the world. I think he's even been to Spain. You've talked about wanting to go to Spain."

The dinner had been a fiasco, with Jimmy asking polite questions, cracking jokes, Cassandra sullen and withdrawn, Graham rambling to compensate. Jimmy never brought it up afterwards, though, never mentioned Cassandra and for that, Graham felt grateful if not uneasily obligated.

Jimmy finished with the college girls, filled his huge mug with Mountain Dew, came back to stand by Graham. "California?"

"Maybe," Graham said. He looked around covertly. "I just found out I might have a daughter there."

"You shitting me?"

Graham shrugged. "I worked out there right after college."

"They coming after you for child support?"

"Hasn't gotten that far yet."

Jimmy slurped at his Mountain Dew, deep in thought. "Well. Make sure you take a test. Could be a major scam."

"I don't understand," Cassandra said. "Why don't you try to find out for sure before you go all the way out there?"

They were upstairs, in Graham's room. He was packing.

"How?"

"Call and ask. Call her mother."

"They'd lie. If they wanted me in the picture they would have contacted me."

"You could hire someone. A private detective."

"Give me a break."

"It would be exciting. Like the *Rockford Files*."

John Salter

Graham laughed. "Hire with what? I barely make minimum wage."

"We'll save up. I'll get rid of my cable."

"No. That could take months and I don't want to wait any more. Who knows what's going on out there? What kind of life she might have?"

"She?"

"He. She. Whatever." He turned away to zip his travel bag; when he turned back, Cassandra was gone. It was raining again, very lightly.

Cassandra was outside, leaning against the house, smoking. The smoke didn't rise; it traveled away from her low to the ground like a winding, fog-shrouded river. She was crying. Her bony shoulders quaked. "Look," Graham said, reaching out to pat her arm. "Everything will be okay. I'll be back in a week or so. I have to be back at the store in ten days at the latest."

She squirmed away from him.

"Jimmy said you can call him if you get in a bind."

She closed her eyes. "It's not your daughter. It was just a nonsense dream. I don't know why I said that."

"I have a responsibility," he said. "I have to see about this."

She turned, pressed her forehead against the chipped clapboards.

Grand Forks, a city without much influence on the horizon, disappeared quickly in Graham's rear-view mirror. He brought the Thunderbird up to seventy and rolled down the window, sang along to Van Morrison's "Brown-Eyed Girl." He honked and waved at a farmer in a big John Deere tractor. He realized with a start that he had not been farther than the edge of town in almost three years. He passed Thompson, then Reynolds, Buxton. When he flew over the railroad bridge near Hillsboro, the most significant curve and only hill on the way to Fargo, he shivered, and a great exhilaration swept into his chest. He grinned like a fool. He knew it was hopeless but he hoped anyway that unlike heroin or a dream he could make the feeling last awhile.

THE BEAR'S FOURTH LEG

The Rural Mail Carrier was weeping when he hit the boy.

There were other factors. Blaze of eastern sun on the dusty windshield, loud music—Rod Stewart's "Maggie May"—bundles of mail crowding him against the door.

A shadow and a bump.

A shadow, a bump, and the boy flew across the ditch and snagged like torn paper in the drooping barbed wire.

Birds exploded from the tall weeds along the fence.

They found some things around the dead boy. A school copy of Jack London's *The Call of the Wild*, a plastic bag of mushy ground beef, a cheap pocketknife featuring a spoon and fork. The tool was so old that when a deputy examined it while waiting for the coroner to arrive, one of the fork's tines fell off. The metal was fatigued. The deputy glanced around, refolded the knife, and walked over to stand by the other deputy, who was smoking a cigarette and looking at the Jack London. "I can't believe it. This was one of my favorite books in junior high."

"Hmm."

"You ever read Jack London?"

"No. I wish they'd get here."

"I haven't read this book in I don't know, something like what? Thirteen, twenty-three, thirty-three. Twenty years? That can't be. No that's right. Twenty years."

"Look at his shoes. Look how beat-up they are. Imagine dying in old shoes like that."

"Twenty years? Jesus."

The dead boy's mother kept dropping glasses but the men in the bar that early in the day were immune to the shock of noise. One two three glasses in two hours. She made a pot of coffee and dumped it out five minutes later thinking it was old. She lighted a cigarette and placed it in an ashtray and a few minutes later, after re-supplying the men, she lighted a second cigarette at the other end of the bar. She looked down at the first cigarette, the feeble breath of the nearby alcoholics too impotent to have an influence on the smoke rising in a perfectly straight column.

The Rural Mail Carrier's lunch: crunchy bean sprouts and lean turkey on coarse rye. His wife read *Prevention* and fretted over his colon, his prostate, his spine. He had nothing to wash the sandwich down with but the remains of his watery morning coffee. The Postmaster always made the coffee weak. They'd argued about it one morning and the other carrier said they sounded like an old married couple and the Rural Mail Carrier had resolved at that moment to never get into it with the Postmaster again.

He sat on the hood of his car, chewing slowly. He regarded the front right fender, the atlas of scratches from brush-lined driveways, inappropriately planted mailbox posts.

A shadow.

A bump.

He slid from the hood and walked up the road a few yards. Stopped. Scuffed around on the gravel shoulder. He turned his back to the car and stared at the long stripe of blacktop, the shimmering mirages. The Rural Mail Carrier began walking along the road, slowly, trying to remember how he'd walked as a boy. He pretended to bounce a ball as he walked. He glanced back at his car. Walked a little more. Glanced back at the headlights.

He snapped his fingers.

At home, the deputy who'd read Jack London took off his uniform in the bedroom and hung his pants on a hanger, paying particular attention to the creases so he wouldn't have to iron in the morning. He buried his pistol in his underwear drawer. He dropped his socks and shirt in a heap. He pulled on a University of North Dakota sweatshirt and jeans and slipped running shoes over his bare feet. He went to the kitchen for a beer and carried it through the door into the garage. He had a little area for smoking in the garage, a lawn chair and a table he'd made. The table had three legs and narrow planks forming a triangular top that gave it a vaguely aeronautical presentation. The deputy had made the table for his wife to put on the deck but a week later she'd gone out and bought a plastic table and put his in the garage.

He thought about that, now. There was nothing wrong with

The Bear's Fourth Leg

the table. It wasn't perfectly level but the tilt would have helped runoff during rain. It was rustic. The table had character.

It didn't match the other furniture, his wife had explained.

The dead boy's mother stood in the bathroom removing her smeared makeup. In the corner of the mirror she could see the deputy who broke the fork getting dressed. He finished except for his shoes, which he held pressed together in his lap. He seemed awfully concerned with his shoes. "Do you have any black shoe polish?"

"Do I have any black shoe polish? No I don't have any shoe polish."

She watched the deputy look around as if he'd forgotten where he was, forgotten embracing her, comforting her, forgotten fucking her quickly and greedily. He held his shoes up and squinted at them.

He used the corner of her afghan to shine them.

The evening news carried the report. The Sheriff, grim and fatherly, worried about finding a suspect. It would be tough without witnesses. He wouldn't say if they had any leads.

The Rural Mail Carrier ate his dinner on a tray across his lap while his wife knelt by his feet, clipping his toenails. "Shame on whoever did that," she said.

"Terrible."

"How could someone do that? Run over a little boy and keep going."

"You hit a dog once and kept going. Remember? When we were looking for my cousin's house in Wisconsin?"

"That's different. That's a dog. That's an animal. People aren't animals."

"Some of them are."

"Nonsense."

"Spend a little time in a ghetto."

"Oh you."

"I deliver their mail."

"To the ghetto? In Minnesota? How you talk."

"No. The dead boy."

The Rural Mail Carrier's wife scooped up toenail clippings and dropped them into a crystal ashtray unused except for purposes like this. She squirted lotion into her palm and rubbed her hands together to warm the lotion before applying it to her husband's feet. She was from Russia. The Rural Mail Carrier had ordered her from a catalog he'd plucked from the recycling container at the Post Office. The catalog was addressed to an old sugar beet farmer who'd suffered a stroke and was placed in a nursing home in Moorhead. The catalog was bulk mail and couldn't be forwarded so it had been destined for wherever they took all the recyclables. The Rural Mail Carrier had only taken the catalog for something to read in the bathroom and then he'd seen her photograph and ordered her. His first wife had left him. She was a stubborn, hard woman from Thief River Falls who'd never clip his toenails or even make him lunch. He missed her. She was the reason he'd been weeping when he hit the boy. He regretted pushing her against the bathroom door, which still bore evidence of that terrible night five years earlier—a night when the law had come out, the night she'd gathered her things and left under escort—in the form of a poorly repaired crack that his new wife covered with her bathrobe when performing what sounded through the wood like very complicated hygienic acts before and after lovemaking.

The deputy who'd read Jack London lighted a cigarette and opened the dead boy's book. The boy had drawn on the inside cover the way the deputy had drawn in his own books when he was that age. The boy had drawn an elaborate hunting knife dripping blood from the tip. Below it was a well-done rendering of a long-barreled revolver. Next to the revolver, a bear. The bear appeared to have only three legs. The deputy leaned forward, closer to the open garage door so the light was better. It wasn't a three-legged bear after all. The boy had started to draw the fourth leg but stopped. There was evidence of the dead boy's frustration, failed attempts, eraser marks.

The deputy put the book down and went to the kitchen for a pencil and returned to his chair. He licked the tip of the pencil and very delicately worked at finishing the bear's fourth leg. It wasn't easy. There was a problem with the perspective. He could see why the boy had given up.

The boy's mother talked on the phone for two hours. Her parents wanted to know what he'd been doing playing by the road.

The Bear's Fourth Leg

"He's eleven years old," she said. "Kids here get a driver's license when they're fourteen. Eleven is pretty grown up."

"Still," her mother said. "A boy needs supervision. A boy like that, with problems."

"He doesn't have—he didn't have problems—how many times do I have to say it he had *learning disabilities.*"

"I know, dear."

"Plus he was hyper—he had ADHD. You know how hard it's been to keep track of him."

"I know."

"He wasn't retarded."

Her mother sighed.

She talked next to her brother and his new wife. They lived in Montana. Her brother was trying to be a Montana poet plus he worked full time graveyards at a convenience store. His new wife was pregnant. They'd gone for an amnio and everything looked okay. Her brother was a very emotional person and started crying. "Maybe we'll name our baby after your son," he said.

The boy's mother stared at the boy's gray hooded sweatshirt on the hook by the back door. He didn't hang up the sweatshirt very often. She wondered why he'd hung it up that day of all days. She wondered if that meant something. Then she remembered that she'd been the one to hang it up, when the deputy brought her home.

She got off the phone but it rang a few minutes later. It was her brother again. "About the name," he said. "We'll have to see. I can't make any promises right now."

Three-thirty in the morning and the Rural Mail Carrier was still awake even though he had to get up at five for work. He regarded his sleeping wife's hip. If he shook her from sleep she wouldn't scream at him like his old wife. His new wife would smile and hurry to the bathroom and come back smelling fresh and sweet and lie on her back or get on her hands and knees or kneel before him on the carpet.

He hated her.

He roamed through the house, checking doors, locks, peering through the windows at the night. They lived out in the country. When his children were younger they'd talked about getting a horse but never had. Now the Rural Mail Carrier kind of wished he had a horse. He'd go out to the barn and feed his horse an

John Salter

apple and talk to it. The horse would gaze at him through calm, understanding eyes as big and black as full coffee cups. He brewed a pot of coffee in the Bunn his first wife's parents had gotten them for a wedding present. It took only a few seconds to brew coffee in the Bunn. There was always a reservoir of hot water. He remembered how after an argument his first wife had left for work and unplugged the Bunn on her way out the door. It took at least an hour for the reservoir to warm up so that morning he'd suffered without coffee. It had been the singularly meanest thing she'd ever done to him but he remembered the act fondly.

He poured a cup and set it on the counter to cool. He filled an identical cup and arranged it by the first and squinted. The horse would have a simple name like Buck or Joe or Bonnie. "Pal," he whispered. "It was an accident. In my heart I know that. God knows. I was afraid. I could lose my job and then where would we be? We'd have to move to town and live in an apartment. We could get sued. The boy's mother is poor. She gets Fingerhut catalogs and letters from social services. There'd be all kinds of lawyers involved. What's done is done. It happened like this." He snapped his fingers.

"Who are you talking to?" his wife asked.

She was in the doorway. Her nightgown shimmered. She had a body like a model. Not an American supermodel but a strong, knobby Russian model, statuesque and blond, hands big as his own. "I made you some coffee," he said.

The deputy who'd read Jack London squeezed into a place at the table with his children. He had a headache. It didn't help that his wife's sneakers squeaked on the floor as she hurried about the kitchen. She wore bleach-white shoes at all times. She reminded him of all the wives in the neighborhood. Sometimes she went on power walks with four or five of the other wives and by the time they reached the corner he couldn't discern her from the others. Sometimes he wondered what would happen after the walks if the wives just went to any house they wanted to. He wondered if the women all made love the same way, like Kelly did, like it was an aerobic session and he was just another television infomercial product like her Ab-Blaster.

"How was work?" his wife asked.

"Fine," the deputy said. "I had to unhook a dead boy from a barbed wire fence."

The Bear's Fourth Leg

The deputy's children screwed up their faces.

"Part of his ear is still on the fence."

His daughter said, "Gross."

His son said, "Cool."

His wife glared at him.

After dinner, he pushed back from the table and stood up. "I'm going out," he said.

"Don't forget I have Tae Kwon Do at eight," his wife said.

The deputy threw himself into a karate stance and did his best Bruce Lee howl.

His family shrank before his eyes.

The dead boy's mother felt a widening gulf between her groin and her neck. She tried to fill it with countless menthol cigarettes, cans of beer, a mysterious lone red pill left behind months earlier by a temporary paramour. But the space only widened. Every room she entered she had to leave right away because the boy's presence swelled the hot air. She had not yet cried, either, and this worried her. "I *am* sad," she explained to a photograph of the dead boy holding a narrow fish he'd caught at welfare camp. "But you've always made me sad. You made me sad even before you were born. This is just like the last episode of a TV show. Not a big series finale but the last episode before the show doesn't get renewed, when nobody knew it was going to happen." She wondered if she should call the dead boy's father. He lived in Omaha. He worked for the railroad. He'd never met his own son.

Someone knocked on the door. She went to the door and opened it. A man stood on the porch. He held up a book. "This was with your son when he was killed. I thought you might want it."

She stared at the book. "Why do you have it?"

"I'm a deputy," he said. "I was first on the scene."

"This was the only book he ever finished. Took him almost a month. He had learning disabilities."

"I was wondering if I could see his room."

"Is this for the investigation?"

The deputy looked back at the darkened yard. "I guess so," he said.

She looked at his shoes. They were scuffed and dirty. "Okay," she said.

The deputy came in. He seemed genuinely sad, unlike the

other deputy who, even as he'd wrapped his arms around her in support, had peeked down her cleavage, had let his right hand brush against her bottom, had whispered moistly in her ear. This deputy looked about to cry. He stabbed his finger at the hallway. "This way?"

"That way."

She followed him down the hallway. "Ah," he said, when he reached the boy's room with the skull and crossbones on the door. He shut the door as soon as he was inside and when she tried the knob it was locked.

The Rural Mail Carrier, jazzed on coffee and paranoia, fucked his wife at four-thirty in the morning. She always seemed to enjoy it. Two minutes or twenty, The Rural Mail Carrier's Russian wife had exquisite timing and managed to yield an orgasm right before he did, every time, like drivers who always merged at precisely the right moment.

He looked up at her beaming face in the soft morning light. "Spit on me," he said.

His wife didn't bat an eye. She worked a string of saliva from her lips and swung it down to his forehead.

"No, goddammit. Spit on me."

A dollop splattered against his wild eye.

"Spit, spit. Spitsky. Hawk it up like you have tuberculosis."

The Rural Mail Carrier's wife pressed her strong chin to her chest and worked up a knot of mucous, inhaled through her nose like a wild mustang, swinging her head, and spat. The salty missile exploded on the Rural Mail Carrier's upper lip, oozed into his mouth.

"Do it again," he said.

The dead boy had collected a milk crate full of wonderful things, the deputy discovered. He dropped the crate onto the bed and pulled out a rusty Victor Number 1 trap which he set deftly and placed on the floor. He found an *Outdoor Life* magazine and rolled it tightly and walked it over the orange shag carpet toward the trap. He paused the magazine as if it were the leg of a suspicious coyote, then pressed it against the metal plate. The trap jerked and caught the magazine. The deputy smiled. Next out of the milk crate was an almost complete deer skull. It was very clean and the deputy wondered if the boy had bleached it or

The Bear's Fourth Leg

used the more traditional approach of allowing insects to eat the flesh away. Below the skull, the deputy found a receiver plate from a Winchester 94 rifle. Someone many years ago had scratched the name "Galloway" into the metal. He wondered where the boy had found it, whether he'd looked hard in vain for the rest of the rifle.

He rummaged further. He knew he would not find a Nintendo cartridge or a condom or a crack pipe. He was not surprised to find a collection of longish cigarette butts, some marked with lipstick, in a crudely beaded buckskin bag. He selected a butt and poked it into his mouth, lighted it with an Ohio Blue Tip match, and toyed with the dial on an ancient leather-cased transistor radio.

The deputy who'd read Jack London stretched out on the bed and smoked, staring at pictures of elegant Bighorn Sheep and menacing Grizzly Bears and Alaskan peaks the dead boy had cut from magazines and stapled to the walls.

He kicked off his shoes.

The dead boy's mother smeared on deodorant and washed her face. She sprayed Obsession on her midriff and wrists. She slipped into a kimono, swigged mouthwash and ran a brush through her hair. She sat on the edge of the sofa and crossed and uncrossed her legs for half an hour. Then she stood and went to the dead boy's door and knocked.

The deputy didn't answer.

She knocked again. "Are you okay in there?"

Nothing.

She pressed her ear to the door but heard only vague, static-infused music. She hurried to the kitchen for the butter knife she had frequently used to bypass the lock when the boy was being stubborn about taking his medication, or when he was staying up too late with his strange projects. She slipped the knife between the jamb and the trim, flipped her hair back, and popped the door open. "I thought," she began, and she stopped. The deputy was sleeping in the dead boy's bed, the Jack London beside him. She looked around. The boy's room was a mess as usual. She moved his things from the bed. It occurred to her that she could finally get rid of his junk without protest. The notion made her start to cry. She pulled a folded wool blanket from the closet and shook it open, flipped it over the deputy. She brushed the deputy's

John Salter

cheek with the back of her hand. His legs twitched like a sleeping dog's legs. Like her son's legs often had. She turned off the lamp and crawled in with the deputy, very carefully, and stroked his hair as she'd done so many times with her son when only sleep could anchor him.

Experience with Ravens

Quite a few of us had gathered to watch the Indian on the rooftop. Well, there was the assumption he was an Indian. His skin was brown, and long black hair was spilling like a waterfall from the raven mask he wore. Had to be an Indian.

"What's going on?" A suit asked. He was carrying a cell phone, going beyond the immediacy of having it in his pocket or on his belt. This guy was ready for the call, whenever it came in.

Someone else answered the question. "That Indian is fixing to jump or fly. He may be having doubts, though. He's been up there awhile."

"Should I call the police?" the suit asked, holding up the cell.

"And ruin the show?" I said. I was being ironic but irony is always lost on these people.

A woman behind me laughed, though. Took me awhile to find her in the crowd. There were forty people milling around, contributing to the haze of curiosity. Words were being tossed around like a beach ball at a Grateful Dead concert: *jumper, LSD, crow, fetal alcohol syndrome*. She was about forty, with a sort of lithe, French appearance. Dark hair, a very prominent nose. I went over to her. "What do you think of this?"

"This?" she asked, jabbing her hand at the people around us. "Or him."

"Either."

The suit dialed nine-one-one. "There's some kind of Indian getting ready to jump off the Holloway Building," he said. "Yes. He's wearing an eagle mask with a long, black beak. Yes. How should I know?"

The woman flipped her hair back. "I don't think that's an eagle mask," she told me.

"It's a raven. A raven mask," I said.

"Really."

"I think so."

"Not a crow?"

"Absolutely not."

She laughed. Then a tremor ran through the crowd. We looked up. The Indian was walking on the narrow ledge—at least I assumed it was narrow, arms out like a tightrope star. Some sadist yelled for him to jump but if he heard, he didn't let on. Just walked along the ledge to the end and turned around, and started back. There was a bop, a strut to his movement. He jerked his beak around. Up, down, left, right. Again and again.

"The four directions," the woman said.

"Yes," I said. "I think so."

The police arrived. Four cars at once. Two cops ran into the Holloway building and two tried to move us back. The crowd would have none of it. There was some propriety here—we'd been involved longer than they had. A bottle shattered on a cop car and the dynamic shifted. The two cops retreated behind their car and called for help over their clip-on radios. The woman and I stepped back into the narrow doorway of a jewelry store. We were old comrades suddenly. "He won't jump off," I told her.

"He won't? How do you know?"

"Experience."

The Indian was dancing on the ledge, doing some elaborate jumping moves. He was shirtless and his muscular back was shiny from sweat. An elderly man with a cane paused by our doorway and stared up at the Indian. He regarded us and nodded. "Quite a specimen," he said.

The woman laughed. The old man moved on. More cops arrived. One of them had a bullhorn. "Okay, everybody, let's disperse here. Disperse. Disperse." There was panic in his voice. This wasn't a big enough city for riots to be everyday events.

A few people left, but most of the crowd stayed put. Another bottle whistled through the air. "Experience," the woman said. "What do you mean? Experience with Indians on rooftops?"

"Experience with ravens," I told her. "I've never seen a dead raven. I spent years, in my twenties, backpacking in the mountains, in Montana and Wyoming, all over Colorado. All raven country but I've never seen a dead one. And I don't know anybody who has. Why would it happen now?"

She smiled and cocked her head, considering it.

I thought about those days, the travels, the way evening light falling on a cirque basin could swell my heart, how thunderstorms sounded like furious gods. Now life was pretty much one banal concern leading into another. Weather was weather.

Experience with Ravens

The Indian was on one knee, thrusting his hands toward the sun. A fire truck and ambulance pulled up but were blocked from getting close. "Do you have the time?" I asked the woman.

She glanced at her watch. "Eleven."

I was supposed to meet my wife at eleven. We were in the city to shop, have lunch, run errands. Paula was up the street having her eyebrows tweezed. I'd been at a used bookstore but didn't find anything terribly exciting. The Indian on the rooftop had changed the tenor of my morning, though. He was scurrying back and forth on the ledge now. "I wonder if this isn't some kind of protest," I said.

"Protest of what?"

"Not sure. I don't live here so I don't know what the issues are."

"How can a protest be effective without an indication of what's being protested? How will people get the message?"

"Good point," I said.

More police arrived. A cop shoved a woman who was trying to take a picture of the Indian with an old-fashioned Kodak Instamatic. Two big guys with goatees and ponytails grabbed the cop and flung him up the sidewalk, and the crowd parted to form a sort of gauntlet, working the cop over savagely. The two cops who'd gone into the building poured out of the door again, guns drawn. People started throwing things at them, coffee cups and water bottles. The suit was still nearby, shouting into his phone. I heard the words, "civil strife." The Indian continued his dance, apparently oblivious to the commotion below.

The crowd had trapped us in the doorway. Couldn't have left if we wanted to. I imagined my wife with her sore eyebrows and sensitivity to the sun, eight blocks away, pacing the sidewalk in front of the salon, growing annoyed. Perhaps she'd heard about what was happening. She'd stay away, and she'd expect me to have the good sense to steer clear. The woman was gazing at me. "You're troubled," she said.

"Not by all this," I told her. "I have other troubles."

She leaned against me. When I was a child my parents took me to a petting zoo and I was allowed to embrace a doe. The doe was soft but behind her fur were tight muscles, tendons, a system engineered for leaping, for flight. This woman's arm against my arm, her thigh against mine, brought this to the surface after thirty years. "The mind is so complicated," I told her.

John Salter

"The heart even more so," she said.

We kissed. Her cheek was cool. Her breath smelled like mint, not medicinal mint but fresh mint, gathered at dawn from a creek bank. I could not pull away from her. We more or less consumed each other in the doorway. Even when someone in the crowd screamed and we heard gunshots, we did not part, even when the shadow of the Indian passed between us like a knife blade right before he hit the ground.

Experience with Ravens

BARLEY

An eighty-below wind-chill factor can kill you. Exposed skin freezes in seconds. Throw in a strong north wind, heavy snow, and you're likely to die on your way from the car to the house. This happens all the time in North Dakota. These poor saps are found after a blizzard, frozen solid, often only a few yards from their front porch, unable to see even a bright porch bulb through the blowing snow.

So I thought it was insane that Julie, our boss, insisted on keeping the store open. The highways were closed; they were saying on the radio that anyone found on the streets without a good reason would face charges. Not far to the south, the authorities were trying like hell to find some old woman buried in her car, while the batteries in her cell phone were dying out. But here was Julie saying the show must go on. "Remember our motto," she said on the phone. "We never close. Never. Tough it out. You and Silas can each have a Little Deli sandwich if you want. Just make sure you ring them up and save the receipt so it doesn't screw up the inventory. Call me if you need me."

I was in the office, listening to what sounded like a fire crackling in the background, at Julie's condo. Of course, I had no idea whether she even had a fireplace. God forbid she'd ever invite any of us over. I thought I heard Julie take a drink, imagined her on a sofa, legs curled under her, enjoying a gin & tonic and a movie while Silas and I were starting to freeze. The power had been out in our neighborhood for at least an hour. Exposed to the wind, our old gas station was cooling down, fast. We'd long passed the moment when we could see our breath, and now our feet were getting cold.

Silas was sitting on the counter when I came out. "What did she say?"

"We're supposed to tough it out. She said we could have a Little Deli if we wanted. On her."

"What are we supposed to cook it with?"

"That's a good point," I said.

"We should torch this fucking place."

"Be an improvement," I said. I was walking up and down the aisles, dusting, trying to keep my blood flowing. "I was in the cooler a little while ago," I told Silas. "Believe it or not, it was warmer in there than out here."

Silas shook his head, slid down from the counter. He turned to face the cigarette rack, pulled a package of Marlboros and opened it, slid one out, tucked the pack into his shirt pocket. That was a first. I'd never seen Silas so much as eat a Tootsie Roll without following procedure: ringing it up, paying for it, initialing his receipt and taping it to the side of the register. That was why I liked working with him. I was the same way. Others weren't; it made me jumpy being on shift with thieves or slackers.

"Did Julie say how long we're supposed to wait?"

"Nope."

"Typical," he said. He lighted the Marlboro from the candle we had burning on the counter. We weren't supposed to smoke in the store, at least not out front, but during a storm, rules change. Like martial law. We hadn't had a customer in three hours, anyway.

We stared out the window at the blizzard. Our competition across the street flew an American flag and it was now almost invisible. Only occasionally did the wind shift enough to allow us a glimpse of it. While we stood there, the top grommet ripped away from the pole, and the flag flapped wildly, like a kite's tail. Then it disappeared again behind a wall of snow. A few moments later there was another shift in the wind. The flag was gone. "Son of bitch," I said.

"What?"

"You see that?"

"See what?"

"Their flag blew away."

Silas shook his head. "Didn't notice." He drew hard on his cigarette, inspected it, walked over to the door. "I'm going to start my car. Want me to do yours?"

"Sure," I said. "You get them started and I'll go out in awhile and shut them off."

He zipped up his jacket, pulled on his gloves. I tossed him my keys and he was out the door. I poured a cup of cold coffee and watched him run like hell to my car, almost slipping on the ice, and swipe some snow off the door with his arm before pulling it open and diving in. There is no lee side to anything in a North Dakota blizzard. The wind may come from the north but it sucks around buildings, spins cars on the highways. There is nowhere to park to keep a car sheltered except in a garage and then you run the risk of having several feet of snow not drifting as much as *packing* against the door. You're screwed either way.

I was worried my old beater wouldn't turn over but then I saw black smoke shoot from the tailpipe. Silas waited to make sure it didn't die, then jumped out and ducked his head down and ran over to his pickup, parked like always by the dumpster because he was efficient and always waited to take out the trash until he was punched out and on his way. Saved a trip. He could just drop it in the dumpster and climb into his pickup and go off to his apartment by the university, a little studio apartment made smaller from the hundreds of books stacked like the Manhattan skyline along the wall. There was an organization to the piles, but I couldn't pick up on it the one time I saw his place. He'd walked to work that day, something like four miles, after his truck wouldn't start. I gave him a ride home and when we got to his place he invited me in for a beer and we sat at his kitchen table, both of us staring out the window in the general direction of Minnesota and not saying anything until my beer was gone and I told him I had to be getting home to my wife. Silas lived alone. Once in awhile he alluded to an ex but I think it was an ex-girlfriend rather than an ex-wife, someone named Candy who apparently still ebbed into his life occasionally. On certain nights he bought condoms before punching out but not often enough to suggest he needed them regularly. That was all I knew about Silas, that and the fact that he had, years earlier, worked in Montana, something he mentioned every year when fall turned into winter. "There's nothing prettier than fresh snow in the mountains," he'd say. Three years working together and I still had no idea what he'd done in Montana, or why he'd come back to North Dakota.

I was warming my hands over the candle when we had a moment of hope, a brief flicker when all the machinery fired up again: the refrigerating units, the hot dog roller grill, the cash registers. You don't know how much noise you're exposed to in a convenience store until it comes on all at once. "Finally," Silas said. And then it stopped, even before the florescent lights had a chance to fire up.

"Maybe we should call Julie again," I said. "This is ridiculous."

He nodded. I picked up the phone, dialed Julie. The line was busy.

After the cars had been running for a half-hour or so, long enough to get their circulations flowing and heat the batteries, I went out to shut them off. The wind had picked up, if that was possible. There wasn't any traffic on Agassiz Road, normally the second busiest intersection in the state. My face went numb immediately and the wind sucked my breath out. On the news the night before, the weather guy had slipped outside the station and thrown a cup of hot water into the air, and it had frozen immediately, popped and cracked before it hit the ground. I could barely get Silas's door open. The heater was on full-blast but the interior was frigid. I turned off the engine and went to my car, an old Nova I'd inherited from my grandfather. We had another car, my wife and me, a newer Toyota, but she refused to let me take it out in bad weather. I thought about that when I found out the Nova had shut down by itself. With the ignition turned on and the defroster on, the battery had gone dead. I tried to start it again but there wasn't enough juice.

"Well, that happens," Silas said, when I went back inside and told him. "I'll give you a jump later on. Otherwise I'll give you a ride."

"So," I said. "Life in the north, right?"

"Keeps out the riff raff," Silas said. The door opened. After going so long without a customer, we both jumped. A short man who looked like a snow-covered boulder, gray-faced and squinty-eyed, stomped his boots on the floor where I'd just mopped. "You order this shit?" he asked, gesturing at the window.

We stared at him.

"I need a box of barley."

"Barley?" Silas asked.

"The wife needs it. She's making soup."

"A box of barley?"

The man nodded. "Supermarket's closed."

"We don't have any barley," I told him.

"What do you mean?"

"This is a convenience store, sir," Silas said.

Barley

"You don't have any barley?"

"We've got cigarettes," Silas said, deadpan. I couldn't tell if he was joking around or not. "We've got cigarettes. We've got aspirin, motor oil."

"No barley?"

"Not a single grain." I said.

"Hells bells," the man said. He turned around abruptly and marched out the door. Through breaks in the wind we watched him trooping across the street to our competitors. Not more than fifteen seconds later he emerged, started up Agassiz toward the Seven Eleven.

Silas shook his head. "That's why I'm not married."

"At least she cooks for him," I said, but Silas didn't hear or pretended not to, just kept staring out the window, leaving me to laugh at my own effort.

He walked over to the door, started sweeping snow from the man's boots into a pile. Like me, Silas preferred things neat. We kept the store spotless. My wife couldn't understand why. "They don't pay you crap and you do all this extra. Nobody else does." Or: "You bust your ass to keep that gas station clean but you can't lift a finger around here. Why is that?"

An hour later, power had come on but the heater was taking its time, clicking and shaking. Outside, the blizzard was showing no sign of letting up. The radio said not to expect conditions to improve until morning, if then. The temperature was twenty-eight below and still dropping. Inside we could still see our breath. The phone rang; the first time all day. A woman with an edge to her voice said, "I'm looking for my husband."

"He's not here. We have no customers in the store right now."

"I sent him out for something an hour and a half ago. We live just down the street and he hasn't come back yet."

"Well," I said. "Maybe his car got stuck. They're not really recommending any travel."

"He was on foot. I sent him to the supermarket but I just called there and they have a recording saying they're closed. Why are they closed? Don't they know that people need things?"

"Probably because of the blizzard," I said. "Everything is closed, just about."

"I sent him out for barley. I can't make soup without barley, you know."

John Salter

I didn't tell her we'd seen him. "I'm sorry," I said. "I can't help you. Maybe you should call the police."

"The police? Why in the name of God would I want to call the police? We only live on Audubon."

"Well," I said.

"What am I supposed to do?" she shrieked. "I have soup started and no barley."

"Good luck," I said. She was still squawking when I hung up. I told Silas about the call when he emerged from the cooler, where he'd been re-rotating the milk, a job screwed up regularly by the other employees.

"Sorry bastard," he said.

"Fucking barley," I said.

He nodded back at the cooler. "How hard is it to put the old milk in front? What gets into people, anyhow?"

Phil, the night man, rolled in at exactly eleven o'clock. This was testimony to the rage of the blizzard since he normally showed up an hour early to read the paper and jolt up on caffeine before beginning eight hours of pure sloth. Silas and I were already punched out and waiting by the door. Phil furrowed his brow, looked around. "It's cold in here."

"No heat all day," Silas said.

"We left you half a candle, partner," I said.

We bolted into the night. The pickup was running roughly, covered with snow like a shallowly hibernating bear. The heater was on but it was cold inside, and the windows fogged up right away. I looked at my dead car as we pulled out of the lot.

Ahead on the street, I saw a scrap of cloth flapping from a snowdrift. I thought at first it was our competitor's American flag but when we drew closer, I recognized the barley man's coat. Through the blasting snow I thought I saw a curled hand reaching for sky. It might have only been my imagination. But Silas swerved in a way that told me he'd seen something, too.

"Shit," he said.

"You're telling me."

He slowed, pulled into the Motel 76 parking lot, put the truck in reverse. "We have to go back."

I nodded.

He gunned the engine; the tires spun freely over the snow before catching and jerking us back up the street. We passed the barley man again. I looked at Silas. He reached into his shirt pocket, pulled out his Marlboros, held them up. "I can't believe I forgot to pay for my cigarettes," he said.

John Salter

THE INVINCIBLE

"Well, I have a gun, too," Barclay told his wife on the phone. "So maybe *he* better be careful."

She'd called him to say the neighbor across the alley had threatened her. Well, not her so much as Barclay. Evidently, when Sally was in the back yard, trimming the spirea, Spicer walked up and accused Barclay of spying on his wife. Peeping was the word he'd used, according to Sally.

"Did he mention guns specifically?" Barclay asked her.

"Not per se. But he was mad. And I know he has guns." Barclay heard her light a cigarette, inhale. She was upset. She had asthma and only smoked when she was upset, which didn't make a whole lot of sense to Barclay, but what did, in a world where neighbors threatened you over nothing? She kept her cigarettes in the same inlaid oriental motif box in which she kept her diaphragm. She didn't know that Barclay knew the cigarettes—Salems—were in the box. "Mr. Spicer said he'd take care of the problem if you didn't stop."

"That's exactly what he said?"

"Yes. The quote problem unquote. He meant you, I think. I think he meant you."

Barclay was at the office, getting ready for a meeting. He could see the others moving past his door, carrying file folders, coffee cups, on their way to the meeting. Suddenly he couldn't remember what the meeting was about. Risk management? Goal-setting? Spicer was a big guy, worked with his hands, came home at six every night carrying a red cooler. Barclay imagined him at lunch, loading huge sandwiches into his mouth, masticating like a beast, deliberately, thinking about his wife, about Barclay. Phil Barnes poked his head into the office. "You coming or not?"

"I'm coming."

"What?" Barclay's wife asked. He saw her then, her frail waxy hands, her droopy behind, her pinched nose. Contained anxiety, Sally was.

"I'll talk to you later," Barclay said.

It wasn't necessarily polite but it certainly wasn't peeping. You wear a bikini in the yard, you're asking to be looked at, Barclay decided, flopping his legal pad onto the table in the conference room. Get real. You're asking for attention. He looked around at his colleagues. "Barclay is here," he announced.

Barclay and Phil went for a beer after work. They went to the Cowboy Bar, which sounded rough but wasn't, or like a gay bar, which it wasn't either. The Cowboy Bar was in a strip mall, in between a Kinko's and a Hallmark. There were hats and boots on the wall, antique guns, saddles, lots of brass and wood. But the people were basically people like Barclay, like Phil, people in suits and ties, stopping off for a cold one before going home. They went there more or less because Barclay didn't want to go home just yet, and Phil never wanted to go home anymore. "Jesus," Phil said. "The guy threatened Sally? With a gun?"

"He has guns," Barclay said. "He's a hunter. Someone told me he went out west last year and shot a mountain lion with a pistol. They used dogs to tree the mountain lion and then he shot it with a pistol."

"That sounds real sporting," Phil said. He leaned close, glanced around conspiratorially. "So, come on. You and this guy's wife. Huh?" He waggled his eyebrows.

"There is nothing going on," Barclay said. "She was mowing the lawn in her bikini and I glanced over and she saw and whined to her husband."

"She good looking?"

"I guess."

"And now he's going to kill you."

Barclay shrugged. "I guess so."

Phil laughed. He had recently started seeing a girl, a twenty year old, and was full of himself, full of laughter, always wanting to throw his arm around Barclay, punch his shoulder, like they were on the same high school football team and not just managers of a regional store chain. Well, he said. "If you aren't at work Monday morning we'll know what happened."

Spicer did something with cement for a living. Barclay had seen him once, he thought, downtown, with some other men, using long poles, like giant squeegees, smoothing out fresh cement. Barclay was in traffic and could only watch for a few minutes but it was mesmerizing, the way they worked together as if choreographed, pulling the rough, lumpy mess into something smooth and level. One of the men had sported a lime green bandana on his head, like one he'd seen Spicer wearing when he worked in his yard. Lots of people wore bandanas on their heads but normally they were red, maybe blue. So Barclay was pretty sure it was Spicer. Then the light had changed and Barclay had moved on.

Mrs. Spicer didn't normally mow the lawn. They usually had their son do it, a wiry crew-cut boy who'd flipped Barclay off when Barclay refused to pay him twenty dollars to shovel snow. The boy, with the fitting name of Buck, had turned back at the street, holding his shovel the way a tired soldier might hold a rifle, in both hands, arms straight down. "Some of us have to work for a living," he'd shouted at Barclay.

"I'm sure it wasn't a commentary on your career," Sally had told him later, when Barclay was trying to decipher the comment. "I think he was just trying to lay a guilt trip on you."

"You're probably right," Barclay had said, and he meant it. Still, it bothered him more than it should have that a fourteen-year-old would think ill of him because he worked behind a desk. Buck's comment, too, had brought back an unpleasant memory: Barclay's father, moderately high on martinis, complaining that Barclay didn't actually do anything. *You go to work and what? Push air around a table with your what—your colleagues? I'm not saying you should build a house or write a novel because that's not you but Jesus, if you died right now, what would you have? At your funeral you'd have some twerp pretending to cry while inside he's swelling, singing joy to the fucking world because he's getting a promotion.*

Barclay's father was a retired professor, Anthropology, and his efforts had helped some Indians in northern California to relearn their customs, whatever they were. Basketmaking or something, Barclay thought. *I can go out there right now and they'll remember me, treat me like a king. I haven't been there since sixty-eight but that's enough for me. Kids out there can speak the language because of me and that's plenty to look back on, son. Son? Do you see what I mean?*

He called his wife from the Exxon station near their house.

The Invincible

"Where are you? Why are you so late?" Sally asked.

"I had a beer with Phil."

She sighed. "Honey," she said.

"What? I'm not entitled to a beer?"

"You are entitled."

"Thank you. I work hard, you know."

"I know you do."

"I get tired."

"I know you do."

"And I sure as hell don't need some redneck trying to kill me."

"Nobody's trying to kill you. I don't think he'd kill you."

"I wasn't even looking at his stupid wife."

Barclay heard a sitcom in the background, a laugh track.

"What?" Barclay said.

"Well," she said. "I mean, even if you were, I guess there isn't any law against it. You would have been looking, that's all."

"So what are you saying?"

"He said his wife was pretty upset."

"Hey, I better go."

"Go where? Where are you now, anyway?"

"At the Exxon. I had to pee and I thought I'd call you and now you're treating me like a criminal."

She started to say something but Barclay hung up.

Mrs. Spicer, was her name Danielle? He couldn't remember. They'd waved politely at the Spicers but never formally met. Two years in the neighborhood and Barclay still didn't know entirely if it was Jenson on their right and Olson on the left or vice-versa. At what point, he wondered, pulling into traffic and speeding up, did neighbors stop being neighborly? Maybe it was the transient quality of life in the nineties, people moving around, job to job. When he was growing up, Barclay had attended five different grade schools, but that was rare back then. People asked if his father was military, that's how rare it was. Now the highways were plugged with U-Haul trucks. Barclay and Sally had decided they'd stay put in Minnesota. The children were happy with their yard, with being able to rollerblade down the street, happy with their school. Barclay's daughter was going out for basketball in the fall and he'd promised to install a hoop over the garage. Now he fantasized about renting his own truck and loading them up in

John Salter

the dead of night. Let Spicer wake up at five or whatever ungodly hour he rose and look out and see unblinded windows, excess junk on the curb. Would he feel victorious? Disappointed? Or just surprised?

So what if he'd looked at Mrs. Spicer? You wear a black bikini to mow the lawn, you bend over to pick up rocks and twigs, you reach back and deftly pluck fabric from your butt crack, smooth out the bikini bottom, adjust your boobs before climbing back on, well. Anyone would pause to look. Not just him. Not just a man. Anyone would.

Barclay went to Wal-Mart. He needed shaving cream. He got a cart and pushed it down the racetrack-like main aisle. A young family with unruly twins was going the wrong way down the aisle. As he went around them, Barclay overheard the mother threatening her children with something she referred to as "the underarm pinch." It seemed to work; the children went docile, at least as long as Barclay was in earshot. So that's where it begins, he thought. He imagined Spicer as a small, chunky boy, getting threatened, perhaps beaten, becoming a school bully, a football player no doubt, now a brute.

He turned the corner, went up to sporting goods. He looked at the guns. He owned a gun, a battered .22 his father had given him as a boy. His father had been a hunter in his younger days and wanted Barclay to have the opportunity to follow suit, though he never pushed the matter. For awhile, Barclay had enjoyed taking the .22 to the local dump and shooting at bottles, porcelain sinks, and once, a rat which had stood on its hind legs and done something resembling an obscene gesture before falling over, mortally wounded although it seemed to take forever for the end to arrive. He'd been relieved when his own son, Jerald, showed no interest in hunting. The rifle he kept in the closet though he had not fired it in many years, moving it from his parent's house to his first apartment, then to college housing after marrying Sally. From one squalid apartment to the next, the trailer, now their big ranch house, the rifle had traveled with them, mute witness to their progress, sentry to their fights, hidden when the children were younger, checked on when danger was in the air, though Barclay had never even bought cartridges for it.

Through a glass case he studied hunting knives, no longer the fixed-blade leather handled blood grooved weapons of his

The Invincible

youth but lightweight folding models with space-aged plastic hilts, stainless blades, quasi-military presentation. He asked the clerk to see a model called *The Invincible*, with a half-serrated blade. The knife felt light as air. "I'll take it," Barclay said.

The clerk seemed impressed. "This is a beauty. I have *The Professional* which is like a little brother to *The Invincible*."

"This is good," Barclay said, hefting the knife. "So light." He dragged the blade over his thumbnail, felt a satisfactory friction. "I lost my old knife."

"They're coming out with a new one called *The Paramount* but that's going to be way out of my league."

"You never know," Barclay said, a phrase he'd learned served at once to pacify and dismiss.

Mrs. Spicer wasn't getting any younger. None of them were. There was evidence that at one time she'd had some real spring to her curves, but she was flattering herself if she thought Barclay was spending much time thinking about her. It was a glance. Well, somewhere between a glance and prolonged glance. Barclay had been on the deck, reading the new John Grisham and drinking a bottle of Grain Belt Premium, trying to soak up some of the summer's last good sun, which had to be taken advantage of, living in Minnesota where winter was a six-month ordeal. Sally was off to the grocery store, Jerald and Amy with friends, at the mall perhaps, or a movie. Rare solitude for Barclay, and it was as always the combination of an empty house and his own near-nudity, suntan oil on his chest and legs, that made him feel a bit, well, not so much horny as potent. So much of his time was spent in a suit or at least cotton slacks and a Polo shirt. He couldn't throw on jeans and a cap like Spicer because Barclay never knew when, out and about, he might run into a subordinate or a potential subordinate. As head of Human Resources he believed he represented the company much more than even his superiors because he was, after all, the doorway to the company. It was the nature of the life he had chosen to be on call, at least in spirit, all the time. He could not remember the last time he'd skipped shaving, even on the weekends. Saturday was dinner out with Sally, Sunday was church.

Barclay went to the library. It was cool there, pleasant, peaceful. Civilized. He went to the periodical section and found a

John Salter

comfortable chair and looked at *Newsweek, Time*. He picked up a copy of *Sports Afield* and read part of an article about hunting Bighorn sheep. The thrust of the article was how strenuous the hunting was, occurring as it did in the high Rockies, how much preparation in the form of weightlifting and jogging was required to successfully stalk a trophy sheep. The article was full of the sort of pithy maxims Barclay liked: *Don't blow a once in a lifetime opportunity because you're too lazy to walk around the block a few times before you leave for your hunt*. And: *The bighorn sheep is arguably one of the most beautiful animals on earth, and you owe it at least the same amount of respect you'd give to a 10K run or shingling your garage*. He dug a pen from his shirt pocket, flipped one of his business cards (Barclay King, Human Resources Manager) and copied down the phrases. He could adjust them later to fit the retail world and employ them in his newsletter column, *A Word from the King*.

He couldn't imagine Spicer hunting a Bighorn sheep any more than he could imagine Spicer in the library. So what if Spicer had killed a mountain lion? Barclay pictured him standing under a tree drinking a beer and joking with his friends just before shooting a terrified lion from a high limb, at close range, the way Minnesota bear hunters hung out by garbage piles to "hunt" bears, which they'd have mounted in permanently menacing positions. Where was the sport? The risk?

Barclay looked at the clock. It was almost nine. He wondered when Spicer went to bed.

It was possible too, he'd done something—absentmindedly—which Mrs. Spicer had seen and misinterpreted. Barclay recalled idly rubbing his slick, coconut-smelling chest, closing his eyes, feeling the sun cooking the oil on his skin, warming his eyelids. Maybe he'd slipped his hand under his swim trunks. Mrs. Spicer had also oiled up, for her lawn mowing. She was tan all year long. It was startling to open your eyes from a half-asleep state of relaxation and see not more then twenty yards away a woman in a bikini. Hard to discern true reality from dream reality. He might have been slightly aroused the way men often were upon waking up. If she'd looked over at the right time she might have misconstrued things, his hand in his swimming trunks, his gaze on her. Timing, he thought. Everything might have been all about timing. Not long ago and not terribly far away a newly married

The Invincible

couple had stopped at a rest area where a killer just happened to be hiding in the third stall of the ladies restroom. He'd cut both their throats with a hunting knife. Speculation held that the woman had been afraid to go by herself into the restroom so her groom had accompanied her. Otherwise only the woman would have been killed. The police were pretty sure of that. Bad timing for a potty break, bad timing for the groom to feel chivalrous. If Mrs. Spicer had glanced over a minute earlier she'd have seen her neighbor dozing on the deck; a minute later, reading again, his face hidden from view by the hardcover Grisham, gripped in both hands.

It was dark but not dark enough for Barclay's tastes when he reached his house. He kept going, past the driveway where Sally's Mazda was huddled like a turtle against the garage. He thought he saw them at the table. Were they discussing him, patronizing him, was Amy calling him a "wuss" and Jerald agreeing, and Sally giggling even as she told them to respect their father? If he walked in would he catch them throwing smirky glances at each other? Or were they just playing Trivial Pursuit? Barclay kept going to the corner, turned, went up a block, turned again. He killed his lights and rolled by Spicer's place. Spicer's big white Blazer was in the driveway but the curtains were drawn tight. Barclay briefly thought about just going up to the door, letting the chips fall where they may. Spicer could push him around, threaten him. Punch him. Barclay reached up and felt his nose, and a spasm of fear ran through his flesh. He was afraid of fighting. In grade school he'd learned playground diplomacy to avoid fights, carrying in his pocket a fully loaded Pez dispenser like a weapon for pacifying bullies. Not that he'd never been hurt. His left hand bore a long scar from fairly recent accidental cut with a knife. He knew pain and thought he handled pain pretty well. Jerald had once hit a line drive directly into Barclay's testicles, which had swollen hugely from the resulting hematoma and required nearly a week of sick leave before he could walk normally, and almost a month before he could make love without feeling any pain. He didn't think anything Spicer could dish up would be equal to that. It wasn't the pain, he'd long ago realized, but the anticipation of pain. If Spicer walked up to him from behind while he was washing the car and slapped him, that would be okay, not so bad, anyway, but if Spicer called his name first and shouted, "Let's get it on,"

John Salter

well, Barclay could see himself begging like a baby, possibly urinating in his pants. It was the damnedest thing.

Out on the highway, Barclay brought the car up to seventy-three, set the cruise control, leaned back in the seat. He liked to drive. He entertained a brief fantasy in which Spicer was chasing him but the Blazer was no match for Barclay's Ford Taurus SHO model. It was a sweet car, forest green, very deceptive because it looked completely nondescript, like something grandmothers and ministers drove, but packed a real punch under the hood. He'd once gone ninety-eight miles an hour in the car. He'd gotten spooked at a rest stop and wanted to get home ASAP. Going ninety-eight had made him feel absolutely acute. A deer on the road, the slightest over-correction, could have sent the car sprawling into the ditch, flipping and shattering. The end of Barclay.

Something else his father had said: *I sometimes wish I'd made you kill a deer when you were twelve and eat its heart like my friends in the Sierras do. You want to see a boy become a man, watch him stare at that bloody gob in his hand for twenty minutes like he's about to die and then take a bite and start chewing on it like there's no tomorrow. He can't go back to playing with toys after that. He's become a man and nothing can ever change that. It can't be taken away by anything society hurls at him. If they did that at MBA programs this would be one fucking entirely different world.*

Barclay pulled into a rest area, parked beneath a dark canopy of lush elms at the far end of the parking lot. He shut off the lights and looked from left to right, very slowly, the way his father had told him to do when hunting. Left to right, slowly. You were supposed to look for a break in the pattern because that break could be a deer, a wild turkey.

There was nobody else around, no homosexual liaisons taking place, no truck drivers snoozing. He climbed from the car and opened the trunk, regarded the spotless carpeting, the neat plastic milk crate in which he kept his emergency gear, his winter survival kit and the goofy wool hat Amy had knit him in home economics. He put on the hat, rubbed at his scalp to quell the immediate itching He pulled back the carpet and found a heap of latex gloves, plucked from a wall dispenser at the clinic while he waited for Sally to recover from yet another anxiety-induced asthma attack,

The Invincible

sparked by her discovery of a pair of woman's earrings in a jar of screws in Barclay's workshop. He'd reassured her that he'd simply found the earrings but not soon enough to stem the attack. He pulled on the gloves now, enjoying the mildly painful snap as they tightened around his wrists. He waggled his fingers. In the dim light his hands looked ghostly, independent of his body. He glanced around and ran, crouching, under the pole lights to the squat little building. He entered the ladies restroom, went to the third stall and crouched on the toilet to wait, *The Invincible* between his teeth.

Sorting Out

The house is quiet. Lund is in his basement workshop, in boxer shorts, sorting a mound of screws and nuts into baby food jars dropped off a week ago by his niece. Lund plans to nail the lids to the underside of a shelf and screw the jars into the lids, something his father did. Lund has been thinking about this for years but only when Carla had her baby and he noticed the accumulating Gerber jars did it occur to him the opportunity was at hand. So now he has eleven spotless jars lined up and he's sorting: wood screws in one jar, washers in another, sharp black sheet rock screws in the third. It is mindless work, but satisfying, like sanding wood.

The ceiling above him creaks. Someone is walking through the kitchen. He hears water in the pipes. More creaking, another person. Then, the murmur of voices. Laughter. The creaking works its way through the house and he hears the shower starting.

Sheet metal screws in the fourth jar. When their father died, Lund and his brother argued over his bolts and nuts, his jars. Their mother, bound for a senior apartment complex, had no need for most of the residue of forty years of marriage. Some bedding, photographs, clothing, a few books, that was all. Everything else had been tossed or divided. When it came down to the jars, neither Lund nor his brother were willing to budge. Their wives had to intervene. Kevin won out by virtue of being the oldest.

Footsteps on the stairs. Lund leans back from the workbench and sees Sandra's feet, then her calves, the hem of her green terrycloth bathrobe. He goes back to his sorting and she appears in the doorway. "I was wondering where you went."

He nods.

She comes over and stands beside him, runs her hand over the mound of bolts and nuts. "Are you okay?"

"I'm okay. I'm fine."

He regards her tan, oily-looking fingers and bright red nails, sees again her nails against Terry's wide back, her hands roaming over his skin as if seeking a hold on a slippery cliff. "How about you?"

"Mmm. I'm fine." She plucks a tiny silver screw from the pile, squints at it. "What's something like this for?"

"When the downspouts kept unhooking from the gutters. I got tired of putting them together all the time so I just used these screws."

She nods. The shower is still running upstairs. Lund glances at the ceiling. "Pretty free with the water, isn't he?"

Sandra puts her hand on his arm. "You coming up soon?"

"Pretty soon," Lund says, not sure if he means it or not.

It's seven-thirty. Lund scratches his belly. He itches all over and doesn't know why. He wasn't itching last night when they arrived at The Plow, a Fargo bar. They'd planned on going to *Titanic* but fifteen minutes into it, the projector broke and they were all given free tickets and booted out the door. The children were spending the night with Sandra's sister, Louise. "Now what?" Sandra asked. A misty spring rain had gathered in her hair, the water dancing on the hairspray she'd used so liberally, readying herself for this, a rare night out.

"You look foxy," Lund said. He meant it. His wife was thirty-seven and he didn't think she'd ever looked so sexy. Something about maturity, the confidence that comes with raising children, managing a home, seeing certain dreams come to fruition and more frivolous ones evaporate quietly, had left Sandra displaying more elegance than wear.

"You're crazy," she said. "Should we just go home? We can watch a show at home."

"No," Lund said. "Let's go for a drink. We're dressed up and all."

"Just one or two," Sandra said. "Anymore, I can't handle booze."

Lund smells bacon now, the aroma ebbing down the stairs and into his workshop. Bacon? Was breakfast part of the deal? He spots a roofing nail in the pile and segregates it, then finds two more. He will give them their own jar, he decides. Three or more of something will get their own jar.

John Salter

But it wasn't just one or two drinks. There was a dart tournament taking place and The Plow was hopping, lots of interesting people to look at. Lund and his wife don't get out very often—lately, it's just a hurried run into Fargo for dinner, a rush to get back to relieve the babysitter. They both felt drunk with the excess of time even before they started drinking, and they didn't pace themselves, so after an hour they were both pretty buzzed, and Sandra stuck her foot between his thighs, and for some reason Lund reached across the table and unbuttoned Sandra's blouse—the top three buttons, revealing plenty of her bronze cleavage. It was an odd thing for Lund to do because if she'd been going out with her friends, say for a wedding shower, and had left the house with the top three buttons undone, Lund would have thrown a fit. For her part, Sandra waggled her eyebrows and spread apart the blouse even more, and it wasn't long after that Terry, on his way back from the restroom to join his friends, walked by and glanced down, first at Lund and then at Sandra.

The water has stopped and Lund hears the squeaky shower door slide open, the thump of heavy feet on the bathroom floor. More voices, muffled, but the word *starving* comes through clearly. Giggles. Lund pricks his thumb on a sharp tack. The tack is an orphan. He throws it into the jar with the other orphans: the nail with a jeweled head—he has no idea where it came from—and the plastic screw anchor, one of a set of two. He used the other to hang a map of the world in the dining room. They owned the map for months before close inspection revealed that it bore words written in Italian, not that it mattered, it was just a decoration, but still, it bothered Lund that he'd failed to notice.

That moment: Terry looking down at Sandra's breasts, Lund gazing at Terry, Sandra staring at Terry's big gold rodeo buckle. Time and motion suspended. Even the smoke from Sandra's cigarette seemed to hang above the table, shaped like a cornucopia with Terry at the mouth. Then Lund saying *why don't you join us?* even as Sandra was sliding over and making room for him, for Terry, who they know but only remotely, so vaguely that Lund still isn't sure if he's Carla's husband's co-worker or Carla's. They met him at Carla's wedding dance, at the VFW. And Lund remembers how driving home that night, hurtling down the highway under a bright moon, Sandra had made a comment about

Sorting Out

that good-looking friend of Carla and Jack's; how she had pinched Terry's rear while dancing and was Lund mad since she was only goofing around and he'd said of course not. But that night, making love, he'd imagined her and Terry making love and enjoyed a ferocity in bed he'd thought had vanished for good years earlier.

Boots now, on the kitchen floor. Lund backs away from the bench and regards his slippers, brown vinyl, a gift from the children, the backs flattened for easy access and removal. His ankles are white. He sucks blood from his wounded thumb.

Terry drove fast, like a cowboy, and Lund had to lead-foot it to keep up with the old Ford pickup. He didn't like the speed, things playing out faster than he could absorb them. The flooded ditches made it seem like they were on a very long bridge, something you'd find in Florida, not Minnesota. He saw Sandra's head through the window, her tall hairdo shadowy in the lights of oncoming traffic, not sitting against the passenger door but right next to Terry on the bench seat. Alone in the big, immaculately clean Oldsmobile, Lund felt like a sailor adrift. Every song on the radio offered dangerous lyrics. His throat was dry. At the turnoff there was a moment when he thought Terry would just keep going, leave him behind, but it was less that than Terry's easy authority over road and machine, and almost too late for safety he swung left and accelerated while Lund was still letting gravity bring him down to a reasonable speed.

Lund climbs the steps, enters the kitchen. Terry is dressed in his cactus-print western shirt, his hair wet and combed back. "Morning," he says.

Lund nods, pours a cup of coffee. He observes his wife flitting around the kitchen, a Mona Lisa smile across her face. She carries her plate to the table and joins Terry. Lund leans against the refrigerator and sips his coffee. Lund never eats breakfast. He's never hungry in the morning. Terry has a mouthful of scrambled eggs but jabs his fork at the sliding window facing the back yard. He swallows. "Pretty day, going to be."

"Beautiful," Sandra says.

Lund nods. "We've been lucky the last couple of days. Lots of sun."

John Salter

She enjoyed it. Terry wasn't bored, either. Lund can't imagine they talked about it on the way back to the house but Terry sure didn't seem surprised when Sandra forced open the pearl buttons on his shirt, slipped her hand inside, rubbed his hairy chest in slow circles while Lund sat in his Lazyboy with a Corona, watching, drunker than he'd been in years—and not even that drunk, not the way he'd gotten drunk in college, waking up in his mother's front yard crushing the tulips—while Terry grinned and squeezed another lime slice down the neck of his own beer bottle.

"We'll have to pick up the kids pretty soon," Lund says.

Sandra shrugs. "I'll wait until Louise calls."

"How many you got?" Terry asks.

Lund springs two fingers. "Nine and seven. Girls."

"My daughter is four," Terry says. "She lives in Wyoming with my ex and the asshole she married."

"That has to be real tough," Lund says.

Terry fishes a Marlboro from his shirt pocket and lights it with a Nascar Zippo. "Good breakfast."

Sandra nibbles at a piece of bacon. "Most important meal of the day."

Terry grins at her. Sandra laughs.

"Well," Lund says. "I have some things to do. You have a good day, now."

"You, too," Terry says.

Back at the workbench, Lund sips his coffee. He turns on the radio. All the local AM stations are playing church services. He switches to FM, country music. It reminds him of Terry and he turns the radio off. The pile of screws and nuts has not gotten much smaller. How has he accumulated so many fasteners in his life? He doubts he'll ever find a use for them all. His father was seventy when he passed on and just look at all the screws and nuts he had left over.

Still, Lund thinks. Still, you never know.

He sorts. He hears the boots, a plate being dropped carelessly into the sink.

The way she turned and looked at Lund, from the bed, close to the finish. Her eyes watery and grateful.

Sorting Out

Lund hears the door shut, the brash Ford starting up, the huge engine revving. He imagines a cloud of black oil-smoke enveloping the house, clinging to the hedges, bringing neighbors to their windows. People get up early in Minnesota.

Lund grabs a handful of screws and drops them into a jar, filling it. He scoops up more fasteners, pushes them into jars. Some are fuller than others are and he adjusts, until they're all equally full. The jars look better that way. Balanced. It doesn't matter how they're organized, he decides. He'll be able to find what he needs when he needs it. It will just take longer, that's all. He slides the jars to the back of the workbench.

This could be any Sunday morning. Upstairs, his wife is starting on the breakfast dishes. The newspaper, unread, will be waiting for him. The grass will need cutting. Later, they'll take the children for a walk, see what the neighbors are up to, yard-wise. Perhaps they'll go out for ice cream.

She is singing now.

Singing.

Lund dumps the jars and starts sorting again.

John Salter

A Clerk's Progress

Thrall liked a little bleach in the water. There was something absolutely clean about the aroma. His girlfriend complained, asked him to at least rub lotion into his hands to mask the odor. One of those issues, he sometimes thought, their impending marriage would eventually swallow, like toothpaste tube disputes, toilet paper roll direction.

He smoked a cigarette while the bucket was filling. The chime on the door wasn't working so he occasionally took a couple steps to peek out from the back room, see if anyone was in the store. The store had been quiet, though, for a few days. Quade's Pit Stop was near the university, which was on hiatus before summer session. Most of the students were gone. Some forever. There was a girl he'd often talked to, a biology major, a tall girl with freckly tanned skin the color of a ten year old penny. She was tall enough that she had to bend to sign her checks on the counter and he often peeked down her blouse, and she often wore loose blouses, and the freckles in between her breasts often left him distracted for hours. But he still looked. Her name was Kyra. They'd had an interesting discussion one evening about genetics, and she'd said if she and Thrall bore children they wouldn't necessarily have brown eyes like they both had. She'd come in that afternoon for gas, her little Toyota sagging almost to the ground, her mountain bike strapped to the roof. "Well," he'd said, the way he had the year before. "See you in the fall."

"No you won't."

He'd been taken aback, worried for a moment she'd seen him looking down her blouse like a teenager and not someone closing in on thirty. "I won't?"

She'd lifted up her sunglasses. "Graduated."

"Well. Congratulations."

"It's just a stepping stone. This fall I'll be in med school."

"Wow."

"I'll have to find a new gas station."

"I guess."

And she'd left. Gone forever, leaving Thrall only shards of regret to handle as he worked his shift.

He turned off the water and dropped a fresh rag into the bucket. There was a note on the shelf, in the manager's loopy handwriting: *Please use rags more than once.* Miranda. He tore off the sign and plunged a hole through her name with his cigarette, then folded it up and threw it away, dipped his cigarette in the bleach water to extinguish it, dropped it into the garbage. He carried the bucket back out front, over to the fast food area, and wrung out the rag. Someone came in and he wiped his hand on his orange vest, went behind the counter. "Yes?"

An old man with infant-thin white hair and glasses was squinting at the rack of skin magazines behind the counter. "How about a *Playgirl*?"

"*Playgirl*?"

"That's what I said." The man looked back at the door, then at Thrall.

Thrall stepped away, grabbed the plastic-wrapped magazine from the rack, checked the price, and punched it in. He didn't sell many *Playgirls*, just now and then to girls buying joke wedding shower gifts. The man smiled. "I like your vest."

Thrall looked down at his vest, too short, orange polyester, a grease stain across the buttons from earlier when he was cleaning the roller grill. He looked up. He couldn't tell if the man was being sarcastic or not. "Can I get you anything else?"

"Are you in the Air Force?"

"What?"

"The Air Force."

"No."

"Were you?"

Thrall shook his head. He thought he'd seen the man before, at the mall, wearing a lime green sweat suit and walking briskly around the edge of the corridors where people walked for exercise when it was forty below out. The man glanced at the cash register and dug for his money. "Young guy like you must have more than one girlfriend."

"Nope. Just one." Thrall feigned interest in arranging the money in his drawer.

"Lots of guys I know with girlfriends still like the occasional blow job here and there if you know what I mean."

John Salter

"That's nice," Thrall said. He handed back change. "Do you want your receipt?"

"What's your favorite drink? Beer?"

"Calvados," Thrall said, though he'd never tried it.

"You like screwdrivers?"

"Not really."

"You want to come over sometime for a drink and a blowjob?"

Thrall glared down at the orange counter. "Not really."

"Sure you do. The man reached out and plucked at Thrall's vest. "That really is a cool vest."

Thrall backed away. He felt his face reddening. "I said I'm not interested."

The man rolled up the *Playgirl.* "See you," he said.

Thrall wiped down the counters, applied muscle to the occasional sticky spot. A blob of dried ketchup required his fingernails. An Iranian student came in. "Man, I have got the munchies," he said.

"You're in the right place, then."

The Iranian bopped up to the roller grill. He opened the warmer drawer, examined the Styrofoam containers. "This quarter-pound all beef hot dog, it is all beef, correct?"

Thrall wandered over. "Yes."

"No pork?"

"Not a bit."

"You sure, man?"

"I'm sure."

The Iranian gazed at Thrall suspiciously. Thrall had once observed the Iranian meeting some other Iranians in the parking lot; the two other Iranians had kissed his hand and deferred to him in a way that Thrall had never witnessed before or even thought imaginable in the United States. "You damn sure man?"

Thrall laughed. "I'm damn sure."

"I see." The Iranian put the box back in the drawer and shut it, wandered down the aisles. He bought a bag of potato chips, a box of Oreos, three packages of Camel Lights.

After work, Thrall drove over to his girlfriend's place on the north side of town. He let himself in. Wanda was sleeping on the couch, wrapped tightly in a blue blanket. Her mouth was open, her nostrils aimed toward the door like shotgun muzzles. The

A Clerk's Progress

television was on. David Letterman. Thrall sank into her easy chair and watched Letterman until it was over, then stood and went into the kitchen and looked in the refrigerator. There was a half-eaten burrito and heap of refried beans in a Styrofoam box and he took it out, nibbled around the edges, put it back. He remembered that she was going to Mexican Village that night with some friends from the hospital, to drink margaritas. He thought she'd said something about how one of the girls was leaving, moving to Colorado with her husband who'd just graduated with a degree in engineering. Thrall lighted a cigarette and poured a glass of stale wine from the bottle of Chardonnay they'd gotten over a week earlier. Screw top. It tasted like bad Kool-Aid. He sat at her kitchen table and thought about what it might be like to be an engineer in Colorado. For some reason he pictured a man in high-top waders, standing in a mountain stream, trout bumping his ankles, using a surveying outfit to measure, taking notes in a waterproof notebook. Maybe the engineer would have a .44 magnum on his hip, in case he ran into a marauding grizzly. He'd have a four-wheel-drive, not a glossy Jeep Cherokee with a child's car seat like Wanda's sister owned, rushed to the car wash whenever it encountered gravel or dust, but a beat up pickup with knobby tires, unattended dents and scratches. Then Thrall remembered that the man, Wanda's friend's husband, was an electrical engineer, did something with "systems." He shrugged and drained the wine.

He heard the television turn off, and Wanda came in, dragging her blanket behind her like a three year old. "Hey."
"Hey."
"I fell asleep. Too many margaritas."
He nodded. "That'll do it."
She came over and leaned down to kiss him. Her mouth tasted like old booze but it was oddly arousing. "How was work?"
"Fine," he said. "Some old queer tried to pick me up."
"No way. Really?"
He nodded. "Invited me for a drink and a blowjob."
"Gross. What did you do?"
"What do you mean, what did I do?"
"I mean, what did you say? Did you hit him?"
"No I didn't hit him."
"My brother would have hit him."

John Salter

"Your brother doesn't work there."

"He would have hit him and walked out. End of story."

"I'm not going to hit an old man. It wasn't that big a deal."

"I wouldn't want you to hit him. I'm just saying."

"Well."

She shuffled to her bedroom door and threw the blanket onto her bed. Then she went into the bathroom. She shut the door. She always shut the door. He wondered if she would still shut the door after they'd been married for many years. He hurried to light another cigarette, took the butt from the ashtray, stuck it in the garbage can, shook the can so the butt disappeared into a crevice. Wanda had been getting him about his smoking. *You'll have to quit when we have children*, she'd told him, like it was an absolute, no room for compromise. Thrall had been taking some evening college courses out at the Air Base, where they were inexpensive and accelerated, and one of the courses, English Composition, had included a section on logical fallacies. The teacher, a man named Hardy, good-natured and eager to take smoke breaks outside, had talked about false dilemmas, and it seemed to Thrall to fit the cigarette situation with Wanda, the proposed children. It didn't have to be either or. There were always porches, garages, windows. It didn't have to be one thing or another.

She emerged, wrapped in her long robe. "I'm going to bed."

Thrall nodded. He thought about Kyra, her slender ankles and calves. Wanda's ankles were sturdier. She'd been a figure skater in her youth, though you wouldn't know it now, Thrall decided, unless when you thought of figure skaters you pictured Tanya Harding and not the willowy Katerina Witt. Wanda had strong legs, muscular legs, though she'd not been on skates in years. Sometimes in bed she locked her legs around his narrow waist and squeezed until thin spider webs appeared behind his eyes. He feared being kicked by her if one of their frequent arguments ever got that far.

He went to the sink and ran water over his cigarette, then went to the bathroom and squeezed a bit of toothpaste directly into his mouth, worked it around, spat it out. He went to the bedroom. She was in her nightshirt, a tattered high school boy's football jersey whose mysterious origin he fretted over sometimes. She was picking her toenail. He sat down beside her, ran his hand over her calf, sent it on a reconnaissance between her pale

A Clerk's Progress

thighs. "Hey," she said. Her green eyes were intent on her foot.

"Come on," he said.

"You know I have to work in the morning."

"How long could it take?"

"Don't remind me," she said.

"Ha ha." He kissed her above the ear, hooked his forefinger over the band of her panties.

"I mean it. Not tonight."

He abandoned the effort and lay back on the pillows. "Guess I'll have to go find that old man."

"You do that now."

"I'm tired."

"I'm more tired."

He sat up. "I want to stay here tonight. We can break the rule." Since getting engaged, they had vowed to not sleep together until their wedding night, a sort of watered down version of the temporary celibacy plan advocated by the Prestons, their marriage prep class leaders.

"Nope."

"I'll sleep on the couch."

"Go away."

He slapped her thigh. "I'll come see you tomorrow at your work before my work."

She kissed him, a peck.

Thrall went, as he often did after work, to the Red Cloud Inn, a 24-hour restaurant near the Interstate. He brought his spiral notebook and a copy of Rimbaud's *Illuminations*. These were mostly props. He'd come to the conclusion that people who sat alone in restaurants for a long time without doing anything productive were generally thought of as crazy by waitresses, other customers. There were a few people like that at the Red Cloud, the woman with the blond wig who recited movies—all the parts, *Casablanca* mostly but sometimes selected portions of *Gone With the Wind*. She wore yards of red lipstick and giant hoop earrings. Her name was Mary. And the man with skin the color and texture of a pumpkin who stared longingly and open mouthed at the waitresses. It didn't matter which waitress.

So Thrall always brought his notebook and pen, could write or doodle for a while, read for awhile, then use the guise of eyesore and intellectual overload to look around, observe people, chat with the waitresses. They probably thought he was odd but not crazy, and that was all that mattered to him.

He liked the transient nature of the place. In his notebook, he'd written *everything is new if you wait long enough*, words that seemed like a poem though he was unsure how to proceed to make it a real poem. But waitresses came and went. One night a beautiful young woman named Regina with jet-black hair and sharp eyebrows, breasts that tested the very fiber of her polyester uniform, had thrown a plate at the wall after getting absolutely flustered by a table of bawdy air force men. She'd torn off her nametag and thrust it like a dagger at one of the airmen, a chunky redhead, before flouncing out the door, never to return. She'd been replaced.

Likewise, because of the proximity to the Interstate, there were always travelers to look at. It was an odd feeling for Thrall, watching the occasional tired couple or solo driver poring over a roadmap, drinking coffee, eating quickly. He saw their cars in the parking lot sometimes, dusty, bug-covered, overloaded with luggage, the dashboards crowded with maps, empty cigarette packages, gum. The cars always made him feel a little envious. Beyond a trip to St. Paul with Wanda, Thrall had not traveled in years. His father had suffered from wanderlust, and they'd moved around most of his childhood. Thrall had gone to three different fourth grades, something he'd thought unique until they arrived in Grand Forks and he met air force brats who could easily top whatever atlas-hopping he'd done. It was ironic, he thought, that the place his father liked least was also the place he'd stayed the longest, five years, until he died of a heart attack, not shoveling a wall of snow as per the cliché but while fishing half-heartedly in the Red River for catfish they couldn't eat anyway due to pollution. Thrall had been with him; his father had grabbed his arm and squeezed, his strong grip close to breaking a thirteen-year-old's bones. Thrall still felt the pain in his arm sometime, halfway between his hand and his elbow, a phantom that arrived without warning, usually at bad times: while making love to Wanda, for example, and once, while test-driving a motorcycle. He hadn't bought the Honda.

The hostess brought his water, coffeepot, an ashtray, and Thrall lighted a cigarette and dropped an ice cube in the cup. Rituals. He opened his notebook. It was less a journal than trapped stray thoughts, but then again, he decided, maybe that was what

A Clerk's Progress

a journal was. His teacher at the air force base had liked his required journal. Despite repeated threats, most of the other students wrote only quick and empty paragraphs about their daily lives. He'd sat next to a woman with short blond hair whose husband was gone to Okinawa for three months. He'd dreamt about the woman and sometimes fantasized about taking up with her while her husband was belly down in a tanker high above the earth, using a tiny joystick to guide a nozzle into a fighter plane's fuel tank. She'd often smiled at Thrall before class, and he'd helped her once to format her research paper citations. He'd felt or imagined he'd felt coming from her a growing burden of lust as each week went by. How do you spell your name? she'd asked, and Thrall had spelled it for her, and later that night in bed with Wanda, not fooling around but right after fooling around, he'd wondered why she needed the spelling and it struck him that she might be writing about her desire for him in her journal, which she always worked in hunched over with her left arm curled around the top in a manner reminding Thrall of how prisoners in movies ate their supper. During the mid-evening break—the class ran from seven-thirty to ten—when everyone poured out to pee and smoke and make phone calls in order to have believable excuses for leaving early, Thrall had quickly flipped open her journal, found the date of her question about his name, and scanned that and subsequent pages for himself. But all he'd seen were the most innocuous of entries: *Kyle threw up peanut butter at school and I had to take him a fresh shirt at noon so I missed* Days of Our Lives. And: *Jim called from Okinawa and said he ate something called cat on a stick but it wasn't really cat, it was something called yakatori (sp?!) and he liked it so much I'm going to try to make it for him when he gets back. That or baked macaroni and cheese.* Hardy had stepped back into the room then for his cigarettes, caught Thrall peeking but only said, enigmatically, "It's what gets left out that matters most sometimes."

Now Thrall turned to a blank page and wrote, *Kyra*, at the top. Right below it: *Wisconsin*.

Below that: *A drink and a blow-job*, which sounded like a good title for a poem or a story, maybe a Hemingway story, but then he crossed it out heavily in black ink, crossed out Kyra and Wisconsin also, and wrote *Wanda Thrall* the way she'd done after he proposed. He remembered finding a steno notebook with *Wanda Thrall* written on seven pages, as if she'd needed to train herself to accept the name by working with it. Thrall had studied Tae Kwon Do when he was eighteen, for a year or so; there had been ways of standing, certain stances that felt unnatural at first, but repetition eventually made them comfortable and even now, years later, he could get into one of the stances and it was like wearing old shoes. He closed his notebook and opened the Rimbaud, picked up at a rummage held by a professor who was retiring and moving to Bemidji to write plays and novels. The professor had seemed pleased he was buying it but refused to lower the price from fifty cents to a quarter which didn't bother Thrall because he'd doubted if the professor had been to enough rummages to understand that haggling was part of the culture.

That had been weeks and weeks earlier and the Rimbaud had gone onto the pile in his car. He was horrified now to see French writing but calmed when he realized the English translation was on the opposing page. He read: *Magic flowers droned. The slopes cradled him. Beasts of a fabulous elegance moved about. The clouds gathered over the high sea, formed of an eternity of hot tears.*

Laughter distracted him. He looked around. Two skinny farmers in baseball caps were giggling over a Far Side cartoon they'd found in an abandoned newspaper. Would they know Rimbaud? He doubted it, but then again, he didn't either. Thrall closed the book and lighted another cigarette. The coffee in his cup was cold but he drank it anyway, not wanting to get a reputation as a pest, although he didn't think he'd be able to come to the restaurant much longer. He was getting married in one month. It wouldn't be right to sit in a restaurant every night with his wife at home. They were going to move Thrall's stuff to her apartment because it was cheaper. They were going to get married on a Saturday and go back to work on Monday. They'd decided to put off their honeymoon until they saved enough to go somewhere interesting. That could take awhile, Thrall decided. Neither of them made very much money. He wanted to go to Mexico but Wanda had never been to Disney World and kept bringing it up. She had brochures. He had no brochures on Mexico. She was winning the information war, he thought.

Three drunk women with big hair showing signs of stress failure came in. Their wake smelled of smoke and booze. They glanced at Thrall, his book and tablet, and one of them shushed the others like unruly children in a library. Thrall smiled at the shusher and she playfully stuck out her tongue at him. Then for awhile, Thrall and the woman looked at each other every few moments, and there was something palpable about the looks, a weight behind the woman's glances, and Thrall believed that something exciting might happen with the woman, and he quickly performed a mental check of his little apartment on the second floor of a listing house, glad he kept it neat, glad he'd made his bed. He felt as if he were in a movie, that he was being carried along by the script. She was statuesque, vivacious. Blond. She wore white diamond-patterned stockings. Thrall wondered what they'd feel like under his palm. He felt dizzy with the possibilities. But a few minutes later the women were joined by three roughnecks at their big round table. Evidently they'd hooked up at the bar right before closing time. The shusher stopped looking at him and put her hand, capped with bright orange fingernails, on the arm of a bearded man with a Minnesota Vikings cap. He watched one of the men drop his hand to his lap and slip off his wedding ring. It fell to the floor and the man spent quite a bit of time reaching down but not looking, patting the floor for it. Thrall wanted to walk over and pick up the ring and hand it to him, present it to him in front of everyone at the table, but he wasn't the type. He gathered his things and left. He didn't want to see what happened to someone else.

John Salter

Og

Her name was Og. His name was Og. They were all called Og, back then. It wasn't a problem. There weren't that many of them to begin with. And if there was ever an occasion when more than two of them gathered around a burning tree or a pool of water, and someone said, "Og," eye contact was enough to differentiate.

But she didn't think about these things. She didn't think about much. She thought about Og. She thought about the cold. She thought about the sun. For some time, she and Og had been traveling, trying to follow the sun. Every morning they woke. If they were colder than the day before, they knew they had gone the wrong direction. Now for several days they hadn't been colder in the mornings, hadn't been much warmer, either, but not any colder, so they were continuing this way.

A bird landed on Og while she was squatting. She watched it circling. It landed on her knee. Looked at her. It was a black bird. Og came up from behind and grabbed it. The bird fluttered and shrieked. Og chewed roughly at its head, silenced it. He held the remaining lump of bloody feathers out to her, and she ate, too. He smiled. She smiled. He chased her through the snow. She tripped and fell, slid down a hill on her stomach. Og slid after her, caught her ankle, gobbled along her calf and thigh, bit her neck. She squealed. While Og prodded and grunted, Og bucked and screamed and pressed her broad forehead against the hard, snow-covered ground.

This mixture of pain and pleasure was for the entire world to see and hear, just as it was many, many, years later when an archaeology professor named Stuart Divine led a petite graduate student named Brianna Dinwoody away from a group working to excavate further evidence of the presence of folks like Og and Og after a farmer named Ermine Nystad reported finding a chunk of fossilized bone while burying his dog, Sandy, killed by a rural mail carrier who'd resented having to deliver a certified letter to Ermine, a task that meant going up the driveway and knocking on the door. Stuart Divine, under the heady influence of pure science, away from the claustrophobic classroom in Grand Forks, breathing fresh air once again, had simply grabbed Brianna's elbow and walked with her, discussing how things might have looked during Og's day, waving his hands theatrically though mostly to disguise his intentions from the other students, who paused in their work to watch one of their own being spirited away for purposes they fully understood after watching weeks of flirtatious behavior and noting just that day that Brianna had applied a healthy mist of Opium before emerging from her tent. They watched Stuart and Brianna climb the hill, saw them stark against the horizon before the pair descended, slowly. No words were spoken at the dig even when Stuart and Brianna had disappeared but a current passed among the students, a flicker of amusement, jealously, contempt.

Og and Og were on the move again, chilly now from the cool wind against the sweat released by their ardor. Og walked in front, chewing on what remained of the bird. Og watched his back, the muscles rippling, shining in the late afternoon sun. Her eyes went up and she watched bugs jumping from Og's head, landing again, jumping. One bug seemed to suspend above him. She hurried forward, tried to swipe it from the air. Her hand went through the bug, brushed Og's hair. He turned, glared. They continued. The bug appeared again. Og slapped herself on the head. She understood this altered her vision. The bug was not a bug. It was something on a snowy hill far ahead of them. It was something coming their way. "Og," she said.

He stopped and turned. She pointed. He squinted. They kept going.

On the downslope of the hill, Stuart Divine looked at Brianna Dinwoody. On a whim, he'd bought a single marijuana cigarette from a pockmarked Indian in Devils Lake and had imagined sharing it with Brianna Dinwoody on the green grass, talking for awhile, making plans for a rendezvous in his tent or hers that night. The marijuana was in lieu of a bottle of wine, which would have been too conspicuous given the other students, would have required tools, vessels. The joint was small and

John Salter

rode more easily in his shirt pocket than a corkscrew would have but when he paused to fish it out and Brianna kept going, his eyes roved down; he regarded her backside, a fleshy study of youthful optimism wrapped in smooth khaki, and her tan, muscular calves disappearing into bulky Vasque hiking boots. Stuart Divine felt far from the excavation, far from the university, far from home and his wife, far not only in distance but, oddly, far in time, eons and eras away from the sweltering confines of the tenure-track box-car he'd been riding in for so long. He lunged at Brianna Dinwoody, dove for her, clamped his hands around her ankles. She fell. He licked her calf. She squealed, tried to crawl away on all fours. He caught her and they rolled together. "Professor Divine," she said. He unbuckled her belt, ripped her flannel shirt open. The sight of her breasts flopping in the cool North Dakota wind was more than he could stand. He attacked her with a ferocity that frightened both of them, and there followed an engagement whose primal sound effects easily carried over the hill and down to the excavation, where the other students stopped their work and listened.

The speck Og had mistaken for a bug became a man. The man was stumbling a bit. Og watched him pause and shield his eyes, obviously noticing them for the first time. "Og," she said.

Og grunted.

The three joined up. The man was thinner than Og and his eyes flashed wildly, roving over the two of them. "Og," he said.

"Og," she said.

"Og," Og said.

There was no small talk back then. Social awkwardness, rare enough to begin with, was handled in other ways. Og scratched at her vagina. Og ran a long dirty finger into his nostril and removed it. The finger was slick with mucous. He regarded it happily, stuck it into his mouth, licked it clean.

The other Og watched with unabashed fascination. Og smiled and dug into his nostril again.

Og sensed something change in the cloud of rank air surrounding them. She didn't know what it was. She had nothing to compare it to. She was aware, suddenly, of the limitations of her own thoughts. This was an epiphany in itself and she slapped herself above the ear very hard to dislodge it from the blunt concerns that occupied her mind. The new Og stepped closer

Og

to Og, very close, and crouched to peer up into his nostrils. Og backed up. Og followed. Og waited for understanding.

Stuart Divine, spent and damp, collected his strewn clothing. Whatever furious possession he'd succumbed to moments earlier had passed and must not, he decided, must not ever visit him again. No, he thought, his future affairs must originate in the cerebrum. This was too zany, too reckless, likely to undermine his authority, even distract him from the important work they were performing at the dig.

Brianna Dinwoody examined her shirt. The buttons were gone, scattered on the prairie. She saw one, shining in the grass like a renegade hailstone, started for it, abandoned the plan. She had no needle and thread. She pulled on the shirt, held it closed with one hand, reached out to Stuart with the other. He was already starting back, his brow furrowed, his face red. "Wait for me," she said. "Please."

He ignored her.

Og chased Og while Og clasped her hands to her mouth and watched. Og caught Og and the two flopped around in the snow. Og bent Og's arm back until Og submitted. Og sat on Og's chest, rammed a crooked finger up his nose, pulled it out, inspected it. The finger was dry. He gave a mighty roar. Og covered her ears. She watched Og force two fingers into Og's nose, heard Og scream, watched the flesh give way. A great spout of blood sprayed Og, colored the snow. Og exploded, pounded Og's head against the ground until Og went still. Og stretched him out, began stabbing his fingers into every orifice he could find, pulling them out, sniffing and tasting. Og ran. She did not look back. Something was happening in her chest, but she had no idea what. She looked for the sun. It was going down. She ran toward it.

When Brianna Dinwoody returned to the dig, still clamping her shirt closed, she understood. She understood as clearly as if Stuart Divine had pecked away at her with his little rock hammer, unearthing, pointing out the ruins. *This is your naiveté. Not much left. This is your love. See, it's been badly damaged, but in the right setting it can be reconstructed. It won't ever be the same, though. Don't fool yourself.* She sobbed. She skirted the dig area,

John Salter

avoiding the glares, the grins, and went to her tent. It was a big dome tent purchased especially for the field trip. She'd also bought two sleeping bags, zipping them together hopefully to create a bed big enough for two, big enough for her and Professor Divine. She had imagined bearing his children, perhaps conceiving them in the tent, not that summer but at some dig in the future, in Mexico or Greece, after she had her doctorate and he had divorced his mousy wife. It was too much to bear now, looking at the sleeping bags. She pulled on a sweatshirt and ran to her car. Her face burned. She drove away from the little parking area Ermine Nystad had staked out, drove over the prairie. When her tires met the gravel she stopped the car and wiped her eyes. She did not go east toward the university. She looked west, saw the sun beginning to dip lower, an old friend, something guaranteed. She drove toward it.

Centuries after Og and Og made love on the slope, weeks after Brianna Dinwoody and Professor Stuart Divine coupled in the grass, Ermine Nystad drove out to inspect the area. The dig had produced nothing very noteworthy, according to Divine, not an old encampment but the equivalent of garbage dropped on a journey, nothing remotely helpful in turning a failed farm into a point of interest for travelers speeding across North Dakota on their way to more interesting places, Disneyland and Montana and New York City. The certified letters continued to arrive, each containing more ominous language, more specific demands.

Ermine slid his hands into his back pockets and, in the manner of his father, his father's father, surveyed his land. Would his son do the same? Would he farm or go to college like the kids who'd come out for the dig? The students had pissed him off a little; they'd demonstrated incredible graciousness before digging, but after failing to hit pay dirt, they'd been sloppy about filling in the hole. Ermine thought he might come back another time with his Bobcat and smooth it out if he didn't lose the farm. He circled the dig, walked up the hill. Just over the top he found a joint poking from the grass. He picked it up, sniffed it, glanced around covertly. He hadn't smoked grass since he was nineteen. It seemed like a good idea now. He sat down, brought out his lighter, and fired up the joint. It was dry as a bone. The same drought that was ruining his farm had preserved the joint. He shook his head.

Og

He saw buttons in the grass, shining like diamonds. There were five or six of them. What was their story? Ermine couldn't imagine. Fucking buttons. Would someone find one in a thousand years and rip the land up again?

He giggled. Crazy world.

SEA-MIST

Shit, we needed the money. Not for drugs or booze, that wasn't us. We weren't hooked on anything but each other. But we had to eat. Pay the rent. And when Sara found the dog we both knew he was a gift if not from God then something bigger than us and Sara said isn't there a story in the bible where that guy lights his son on fire because God or Jesus told him to?

I said I thought it went something like that.

"Was it Abraham Lincoln?"

"Maybe," I said.

Sara well yes she was not so bright but if you could see her fat bottom rolling like the ocean around your thing you'd know my heart inside and out.

The dog was a terrier and the tag on the collar said his name was Seamus. Sara pronounced it See-mus and I liked that, it was like Sea-Mist, something original for a dog. And I love the ocean but even though we're only a few hundred miles from the Pacific I've never seen it in person. I was on my way once, right out of tech school. Got as far as Reno and now all my black Levi's my mother bought me for work are at Dick's Surplus where you can buy them if you want, even buy someone's old underwear if you need it.

Seamus gobbled up everything we offered him, bread and hot dogs and spaghetti sauce. God he was a polite dog, ate like a little man, a little British man, chewed with his mouth shut and licked himself clean before looking up at us. And when he did look up at us he was saying please sir may I have another like that song by Pink Floyd which I understand is based on a classic novel maybe.

We let him sleep with us that night and damned if Seamus didn't act nervous about being on the covers. Kept circling and looking at us like we might boot him off any minute. Maybe someone beat his ass, Sara said. I felt funny about doing it with Seamus nearby but he averted his eyes and only cocked his ears a little when Sara moaned. Sara. What do you do when a whorehouse fires you for being overweight? Her life was so sad it looked pretty selfish to keep going to all the way to Seattle and start a job doing cable television hookups and live in a fine house with my Uncle Dave. Sara's camping trailer with its cement yard suited me. It was fate, anyhow. My fate and hers. Seattle wasn't.

In the morning I took Seamus for a walk around the trailer park. We found where someone's grocery bag had split open the night before and a twelve pack fell out, a few broken beers but one good one, Miller Genuine Draft by the street, and I stuck it in my pants for later. I was the only one awake at seven except for the meth guys in the pink Nashua who always see daybreak but come to it from the other side. Seamus pissed in their yard twice. I think he mistook the ammonia from their cooker for another dog's scent. I moved him along.

Up at the Quick Mart I bought a pack of smokes and we sat on a yellow parking bumper and Seamus gathered smiles and a few pats. It was a pretty morning, all sun. His tail was like a happy little animal riding on a bigger happy animal. The ladies liked him. One fancy gal in a blue dress with a gold Century 21 nametag knelt down to rub his ears and I saw up her skirt. No panties! We all have our daily secrets, like my smoking when we couldn't afford it. Whatever gets you through the day.

At eight-thirty the right car pulled in, a black BMW. Guy was sporting the real Polo horse on his shirt, and his watchband glittered on his hairy tan arm. Too busy to smile at Seamus. Carried his cell phone in his left hand so his time in the store wouldn't be wasted. A man like that couldn't be bothered to make arrangements, get phone numbers, wait for a police report. Man like that would be used to paying for speed, like when I delivered pizzas, before I lost my car, these men who'd say *there's an extra five if you have it here in twenty minutes*. They do the math and calculate what their time is worth. They have loud clocks in their brains.

I held Seamus and he licked my hand. Cute little bugger. What kind of people would abandon such a fine dog? "Who did this to you?" I asked him, and then the Polo man came out. I rubbed the dog tag, thought maybe Sara could polish it up and wear it for a necklace. I was imagining us at a fine place for dinner, Bally's buffet, that tag tucked between her breasts, when the Polo man put his car in reverse and I threw Seamus hard under the turning wheel.

John Salter

ALBERTA CLIPPER

I could go to Paris with Larry Stadstad's wife, Eleanor. She teaches high school art and has wanted for years to go to France, to see the Louvre. Actually, it was a toss-up between the Louvre and the Rijksmuseum over in Amsterdam, she told me, where they keep the Vermeers, but Stadstad didn't want her in Amsterdam because of all the sex deviants. She could say *Louvre* and *Rijksmuseum* properly, with no self-consciousness, and I have to say it was sort of arousing, happening in bed and all. "Name some artists," I whispered, and she rattled them off: *Degas, Delacroix, Monet, Manet, Seurat. Gericault.* Then she got irked because I was licking her ear and said I couldn't have really been listening. Which proves the point that women are women, whether you're married to them or just messing around for the first and maybe only time. It doesn't take long for their womanly concerns to rise to the surface.

Eleanor and I got started in a sort of odd way. I guess there isn't a normal way to mess around with a married woman but I thought it was different. This morning, the temperature was something like twenty-below with a wind-chill ranging from fifty to seventy below. That's cold enough to freeze your skin in seconds. I was at the kitchen table by the window with a cup of coffee, thankful I didn't have to go anywhere because it was Saturday. There was half a beef in the chest freezer, and booze in the house, and my wife, Lacey, had had the foresight to rent a stack of videos from the Food and Fuel on her way home from work Friday night, when the Alberta Clipper was just coming in and snow from an earlier storm was starting to blow across the road and polish the surface into ice. Lacey had picked out some real tearjerkers: *On Golden Pond, Terms of Endearment, Beaches.* She was in the living room under her white afghan, crying, and I was enjoying the closest thing to solitude you get when you're married, and that's an empty room. I was watching the storm kicking up, swirling snow around the garden shed, and thinking about how it reminded me of that story by William Gass, "The Pedersen Kid," which I had to read one summer years ago when

I took a college literature class. I never understood the meaning of the book but Gass really nailed the storm, and I wasn't surprised to learn he was a North Dakotan originally. Then the phone rang and I hurried to answer it because I didn't want Lacey to get interrupted and pause her movie and then get distracted and come into the kitchen and ruin my solitude, which I hadn't really decided what to do with yet. Read, maybe, or work on our taxes, something that can be enjoyable when you don't have too much money to worry about.

It was Eleanor Stadstad, and she was crying. Stad was dead, she told me. At least she was pretty sure he was dead. He'd shot himself. He'd been moody all morning and then went down to the basement, where he kept his H.O. railroad, and after awhile she'd heard a gun shot and yelled down to him but there was no answer. So she'd gone down a few stairs until she saw his legs poking out from under the train table. She was scared to go any farther and would I come over?

"You should call the police," I said.

"I can't do it, Hank. I can't move. I need your help."

"Okay," I told her. I'll be right there."

I went into the living room. I started to tell Lacey what was happening but she let me know through some agitated hand-jerking that she didn't want to be bothered, so I pulled on my coat and boots and went out to the garage and started the pickup. Then I went back inside and got my Iver Johnson revolver from the closet and checked to make sure it was loaded and stuck it into my coat pocket. I've known Stadstad for twenty-five years and he's about as predictable as the weather. When we were young kids going to street dances in little Minnesota towns, Crookston and Mentor, he liked to swing at farmers and start brawls. These assholes are never content to kill just themselves. They get to thinking about how their wife and kids will be miserable too, so they try and take care of everyone at once, best friends included. It's bound to happen at least once every winter in the northland. I love Stadstad like a brother but still, I could see him killing all of us just as easily as I could see that moody bastard killing himself. I wasn't going over there unarmed, that's for sure. I didn't even know he owned a gun. I locked the door on the way out.

The blowing snow made it nearly impossible to see past the

John Salter

hood of the pickup but I've been to Stadstad's so many times it didn't matter all that much. Down the driveway, turn left, stay on the road for exactly three point two miles, turn left on county 18, go two point eight miles, turn right, and there you are. I know the exact mileage because back in the 1980's, we used to jog together. We had just hit our thirties and realized it might take some effort to feel good and stay in shape, so we'd gone together to the Sports Shoppe in Grand Forks and bought New Balance running shoes. A college girl who looked like a swimsuit model had waited on us. Stad had tried flirting with her but it was clear to me she viewed us as old guys, in danger of having heart attacks once we put on the shoes and left the store. Stad and I had worked out a sure-fire motivational plan: I'd get up at six and run to his place, pick him up, and we'd run to my house. Each of us that way had responsibility: I had to get to his place or he'd be pissed off, standing in his yard, dressed and stretching for no reason. And he had to run home or be late for work. This went fine for about three weeks. Then I'd get to his place and he'd suggest a cup of coffee and the early morning would pass. Or I'd call ahead to make sure he was up to it and Eleanor would say he was still sleeping. But when we did it, it worked, and we'd measured the exact distance because we kept journals of our progress, as recommended by the salesgirl. I still have mine, out in the shop, though I haven't looked at it in years.

But in my pickup, in the storm, it took almost half an hour to go five miles. You just can't see far enough in a storm to go very fast. Every year up here, people die in their driveways after getting stuck in their vehicles. They try to walk a hundred yards and get disoriented from the blowing snow, and die. What a mess it would have been, me dead in a snow bank and Stadstad a suicide and maybe Eleanor dead, too, and Lacey wondering what my involvement was after they found me with a revolver. I started wishing I'd filled her in on the details, movie or no movie. That's what a pause button is for, what owning a VCR is all about, isn't it? Being able to interrupt and not miss anything?

I made it, though, it wasn't that bad a storm yet, and parked behind Eleanor's red Jeep Cherokee. I tucked my chin down and headed for the front door, running zigzag so Stadstad couldn't get a round off through the window, though I doubt if he'd have been able to see more than a shadow coming across the yard.

Eleanor was watching and let me in and more or less wrapped

Alberta Clipper

herself around me, all hysterical. I've always had a bit of a thing for her. She has the saddest mouth on the planet. She can't paint and accepted that at an early age, she told me once. To want to have talent and not have it is the burden that gave her a permanent frown. Not that she's unpleasant. She has a sense of humor, she smiles at jokes. Her students love her. Her students all chipped in and bought her a camera to take on her trip to France, a nice Minolta autofocus, that's how much they love her. But she knew long ago that she will never be in a gallery, never be at the Louvre or down in the Twin Cities or even in the coffee place in town. It's a hell of a thing, a real heartbreaker. What makes it worse is that she looks like an artist, slender and big-eyed and dark-haired, and she has hands as smooth and elegant as those owned by the ladies in Da Vinci paintings. Even I could tell you that, with what little I know about art. What a contrast from Stadstad with his electric trains and bass boat. And what a contrast from Lacey with her chubby legs and pinochle tournaments. Don't get me wrong, I love her dearly, but when we used to go out as couples with the Stadstads you got the feeling that people imagined me and Eleanor as married and likewise Lacey and Stad. I don't look all that local myself. A lady professor at the university, where I work as a carpenter, was watching me walk down the hallway about ten years ago, and asked where I was from. Right here, I told her, why? "You have a New England bearing," she said. She taught English. She wasn't bad-looking. I made a point of walking past her office a few more times but she never emerged again. Eleanor had some kind of bearing. When she fell into my arms and I smelled her up close for the very first time and she smelled exactly how I'd always imagined, spicy and sweet, like coconut, actually, I have to say I was a little aroused. Sexually. That sounds awful considering her dead husband and my dead best friend but the truth is awful sometimes.

I held her for a moment and shushed her and told her to wait while I investigated. I stuck my hand in my coat pocket and gripped the pistol when I got to the basement door. I'm no gunman. I'd only ever used the revolver for scaring squirrels, and during the Gordon Kahl incident a few years back, when everyone was on the lookout for fugitives. Beyond that, it had been in the closet, under sweaters I never wore, for years. I started down the stairs and I have to be honest and say that when I saw Stadstad's legs sticking out from under the table I was also wishing I'd see some

John Salter

blood, too. I was still afraid I'd find him only wounded and delusional. I stood there for a while on the bottom step and waited. I had a terrible thought, that if he was dead, Eleanor would remarry. Who would she marry? Some handsome guy who'd been places, seen things, done things? Someone from the university? That bothered me more than my dead friend. I was going over Stad's possible replacements when I heard him cuss, quietly, sort of grunt. "Stad?" I said, real loud. "Stad, It's me, Hank."

He slid out from underneath the table. He looked like hell, hair all disheveled, cobwebs lacing his shoulders. A Ruger .22 automatic was in his hand. My heart started to go haywire. "Hank, what are you doing here?" he asked.

"Eleanor thought you killed yourself."

Stadstad cupped his hands around his ears. "What?"

It would have been funny if Eleanor wasn't upstairs, a nervous wreck. I pointed at the pistol. "What are you doing with that?"

He showed me. He'd wanted to run a wire from a tiny red aircraft warning light on his layout, on a fake mountain. But he couldn't get a drill in between the 2x4 braces under his table. The braces were too close to the wall. So he'd come up with the idea to just shoot a hole in the plywood with the .22. One shot, one hole. A typical dumb Stadstad maneuver. But confined under the table, the sound had blasted his eardrums. He hadn't heard Eleanor calling for him and she hadn't hung around on the stairs long enough to see him moving. "My ears are fucked up," he said, grinning like a moron. "It's like after we went to Van Halen that time."

I looked up at the ceiling. There was a fresh hole in the joist. An inch, either direction, and the bullet might have penetrated the floorboards and gone into the kitchen, and maybe into Eleanor. I pictured Stadstad a widower, on the television news, his dumb Minnesota Vikings hat tilted on his head. *What a freak thing. I'll never do that again.* "Why are you here?" he asked. "Isn't it storming out?"

I nodded. Motioned that I was going upstairs. He pointed at the table. "I'll be up in a few minutes." His layout ran a good ten feet along the wall. Stadstad had worked for a couple years in the Sierras right out of high school, on a crew inspecting power poles, and met Eleanor when she was doing a summer internship for the county arts council, helping poor kids paint a mural. She was from Oregon, originally. She never talked about it, about Oregon.

Alberta Clipper

I think the memory of all that pretty scenery was too painful, living now on the bare prairie. Stadstad's train layout replicated a portion of the old Sierra-Pacific railroad, complete with the Feather River Canyon and plastic water. He'd put quite a bit of time into his trains. He'd go weeks without monkeying around with them but then he'd go downstairs and start working and two days might pass before you saw him again.

"He's not dead," I told Eleanor, when I got upstairs.

"I heard."

"He was using the pistol to drill a hole in his board."

"That's pretty intelligent."

"Well," I said.

"I'm sorry," she said. "I let my imagination go crazy, I guess."

"That happens," I told her.

She looked away. "Maybe it was wishful thinking."

"Been there," I said. "All married people have."

You know those women who can make a jogging suit or jeans look elegant? Not a sloppy house-outfit, but a page from the Sear's catalog, where even the maternity models are stunning? That's Eleanor. She was wearing some sort of black shiny fabric pants and a sweatshirt that said Museum of Modern Art. She'd never been there in person but took their catalog, kept it on the coffee table with her big art books and New Yorker magazines.

"What gets into him?" she whispered.

I shrugged. The air in that house was different. I'd been there hundreds of times over the years but there was something different about the air. I couldn't tell if it was good different or bad different. "Well," I said. "I better get moving before it gets much worse out."

She kissed me. She kissed me and I kissed her. Twenty years without kissing anyone but Lacey and it was like having an ice cold Heineken after being on the wagon for a long time. That sounds hokey but much of the truth does when you get a little older.

She pulled away from me, went over to the basement door. I thought for a second she was bailing out, going downstairs to be with her husband. But she only flicked the hook through the eye, locking him down there. I remembered being over at Stadstad's when he installed that hook, after their daughter fell down the stairs. She wasn't hurt too badly but it was a close call. Stad had been promising to install the hook for weeks and it took an accident

John Salter

for him to finally do it. Twenty years later and I'm kissing that little girl's mother while she's away at Hamline and her father is downstairs playing with his trains.

Eleanor kissed me again. It got pretty intense. Her sweatshirt came off. Her skin was soft as I'd always figured. Her breasts were a little sad, like they'd given up on the future. Things got out of hand and it started to happen, up against the kitchen sink. Any time, Stadstad might have come up the stairs, rattled the door, but he didn't. Eleanor took my hand and yanked me into their bedroom and we finished up there, in Stadstad's bed, with his Vikings cap hanging from the post and his train magazines like stepping stones across the floor. Afterwards, we didn't loiter. We hurried to get dressed. She looked at me. "Regrets?"

"Only that I couldn't take my time with you." Even my words were elevated with her. Like I was in a movie with a good script.

"Come to France with me," she said. "Come to Paris with me next month."

"Paris," I said.

She picked up her exercise pants. My god, there wasn't much to them, like a doll's pants. I watched her pull them on, stretch them over her calves, her thighs. She didn't put on any underwear. "We'll make love all afternoon."

"Well," I said. I was getting aroused again, watching her dress. "What about Stad?"

She picked up a comb from the dresser and ran it through her hair. "Stad won't even take me to freaking Minneapolis. I tried to bribe him with Twins tickets and he still wouldn't go. Paris is out of the question."

I didn't say so, but I didn't like going to Minneapolis either. Neither did Lacey so I was lucky in that respect. I couldn't imagine Paris. The Eiffel tower was all. Rivers. Guys in striped shirts. "Well," I said. "That sounds pretty enticing."

Two point eight miles to County 18 and a right this time, not a left. But in a blizzard, that only works if you checked the odometer when you left Stadstad's place. If you were really thinking you'd jot down the mileage just to make sure. Because what you're doing in a blizzard, really, is driving in a cloud. It's like instrument flying. You make assumptions. You assume nobody else will be on the road at that particular moment. Think of those one-lane bridges out west. You have a choice. Sit and wait forever or go for it on faith, counting on the odds. In a blizzard, if you can, you drive while watching a fence along the road, and adjust accordingly. Mostly you go by feel. You feel the wheels slipping onto the rough along the road and you correct. You go slow. I wasn't going slow enough. What happened back at Stad's was distracting me. You can't get distracted in a blizzard. But when you make it with your best friend's wife and she invites you to Paris you get distracted. My front wheels slipped off the road and I overcorrected, the worst thing you can do. The back end swung around and I went into the ditch, rolled up a little on the right side, came back down. I was stuck. Four-wheel-drive can't work miracles.

Stadstad said something once that bugged the hell out of me. We'd gone into town to look at snowmobiles although neither of us ever bought one. The wives were against it because a boy in Eleanor's class ran into a fence wire on his Polaris and lopped his head off. Afterwards, we were at one of the big nightclubs of the 1980's, Mr. Spud, right across the river in East Grand Forks, Minnesota. We were playing pool with two farmers from Gilby, guys that Stadstad knew remotely from his high school football days. We were all too old to be there but we understood that. We joked about it, joked about these guys our age on the dance floor who didn't understand that, who were swinging their arms, trying to dance to Wang Chung. When the two farmers from Gilby took off, me and Stadstad carried our pitcher over to a table and sat down and watched a group of college girls having some sort of party. One of them kept opening packages of lingerie, goofy sex toys, vibrators. Joke gifts. Maybe it was a bridal shower. Out of the blue, Stad looked at me and said, "I think our wives' names got all mixed up."

"Meaning what?" I asked him.

"Think about it. Eleanor doesn't look like an Eleanor. She looks like a Lacey. And vice-versa."

The music was too loud and it was hard to talk but that was the gist of it. I didn't say anything, just nodded like you do when that's easier than talking. And then one of the college girls threw a dildo at a bouncer and it bounced off him, and people all over the bar started playing a sort of hot potato game with it. But later, I thought about Stad's comment, watched my wife embroidering through thick glasses in the car on our way to

John Salter

Smoky's to eat Sunday dinner. That's an Eleanor, I remember thinking. She is the epitome of an Eleanor. I doubt if Stad had meant it as an insult; it was probably an innocent observation, like wondering why someone might name a Rottweiler *Fluffy*. But it was the truth. There was nothing very lacey about Lacey, while Eleanor would have been at home in a lingerie catalog, not Frederick's of Hollywood but something for the more mature lady, the more elegant lady, a section in J. C. Penny's maybe.

The dumbest thing you can do in a blizzard is leave your vehicle, even to take a leak. But every year people get tired of waiting for help or clearing skies and make a go of it, and die. It would be like trying to swim to shore from a shipwreck in sharky waters. Maybe these people aren't stupid. Maybe dying is better than waiting to die. Every fall, the local news channels brief us on winter survival dos and don'ts. Carry a survival kit, they say. Candles and candy bars, a sleeping bag. Plenty of water. Keep your gas tank full at all times. I checked my gauge. Way less than a quarter tank. I hadn't planned on going anywhere until Monday. You get lazy, especially when there haven't been many blizzards yet. Takes a while to get back in the groove, like coming back to work after a long vacation and you can't make a straight cut to save your life.

Still, I kept my engine running for a while, let the cab get pretty warm, and shut her down. The recommended practice. Run the engine, warm up, turn it off. Conserve your fuel. Make sure your tailpipe isn't plugged or that short nap will last forever. For that matter, avoid sleeping. Play solitaire, read a novel. Avoid booze. A cellular phone might help but Lacey and I refused to own one. We had different reasons. She was convinced that everyone using one would get brain cancer and die in ten years. We'd sit in a theater and listen to the cell phones ringing, hear people talking during a movie, not important calls but bullshit calls about what groceries to bring home, and I'd get furious but Lacey would just smile. "Ten years," she'd whisper. I didn't necessarily believe that, but I didn't like the idea of a cellular phone because I thought it would make me sloppy, like carrying a pistol in the big city and then not paying attention to possible threats.

The wind was stiff enough to rock the truck. It seeped through the door. Maybe the door got bent a little when I half-rolled, but

Alberta Clipper

still, I wondered what I'd paid nearly fifteen thousand dollars for. I started to compose a letter to Ford: *I'm dictating this to my nurse because my hands were amputated after I was forced to spend the night in one of your vehicles.* I don't own a watch and whenever I turned on the radio nobody mentioned the time. They were just repeating the warnings, telling people to stay home. "Only a damn fool would leave the house today," the sheriff was saying. I didn't need that. I shut off the radio. Snow was drifting against the door, spreading across the windshield. Every time I looked it had covered a little more of the glass. It reminded me of those movies where a submarine is taking on water and these helpless sailors watch the level rising. Not too many years ago, an elderly couple disappeared and their car wasn't found until April, in a ditch. People, including their children, had been driving by for months without noticing anything. Finally, when the thaw started, a crop duster out practicing saw a patch of the roof. They had not frozen to death. Carbon monoxide got them. They'd been found holding hands. I started to feel sleepy and cracked the window but the wind and snow swirled in and took my breath away.

You never hear about the wind chill factor in Paris. Does it even snow there? I can't imagine it would amount to much, not like up here in North Dakota. I never thought about Paris one way or another. Lacey never expressed any interest in going overseas. I doubt she could even find Paris on a map. Not that I could, either, without some effort. I imagined a globe, Maine then right to England and glance around until you saw France then Paris. I wondered how long it would take to fly there. Eight hours? Twelve hours? It would have to be a 747. I imagined sitting there under a blanket with Eleanor the whole time. We'd be a couple unless by some chance there were people we knew on the plane. That could happen. You run into people you know in the oddest places. Lacey and I went to Reno once. We were actually supposed to be going to Lake Tahoe but there was a snowstorm and the shuttle wasn't running so we got a room at the Peppermill. We had a card-key that you slid into the door. Lacey didn't trust it but it was all they had. She was afraid there would be a fire and the power would go out and we'd be locked in our room, which was only on the fourth floor but she brooded about it so much I found a K-Mart and bought a fire escape ladder, the kind you hook in the window sill. And a hatchet to break the window with.

John Salter

And a flashlight. On the way back, on the elevator with all this junk, I ran into the professor who'd taught my literature class. He was at the Peppermill with an Indian girl who couldn't have been more than nineteen. He was in love, you could see that. They'd just gotten married at one of those goofy chapels. We all ate a room service dinner together in their room, a fancier room than ours, with a hot tub just off the bed and a mahogany cabinet that opened to a television. The professor's new wife watched MTV while we ate. I didn't ask about his wife in North Dakota. He'd been living in California for several years. Later that night, I went downstairs to play a few slots and the professor was wandering around, all frantic, looking for his bride. I don't know if he ever found her.

I broke another rule. I fell asleep. Dozed off a little. When I woke up the first thing I did was try to start the engine, in a panic. It turned over but wouldn't catch. Too cold, too much wind blowing into the grill, not enough fuel. That was that. Then like a fool, I opened the window again to take a look outside and all the warm air, lukewarm if air can be lukewarm, sucked itself out. Cold air filled the cab. Never get electric windows in the north. There wasn't enough battery left to roll it up, so I was stuck with a partly open window. I laughed, actually. I started shivering right away. The first stage. Your body shivers to protect itself. I read that in the paper after six people died of exposure one winter. First you shiver, then you get numb. Your extremities go numb because your heart needs all the energy to keep you alive. The heart takes it all.

Sometimes when people freeze to death they're found naked, or half-naked. What happens is, your brain gets sort of charitable and tells your body that you're warm. Your brain says, Hey, you're not freezing to death. Christ, you're hot. You're in a Finnish sauna. This highway patrolman I know, Chambers, said it blew his mind the first time he saw it. He'd come across a car the day after a blizzard, when the interstates were closed and people weren't supposed to be driving anyway. There were three dead people in the car, Malaysian students who'd been on their way back to Grand Forks from Winnipeg, where a lot of foreign students go to feel more at home. These Malaysians had gone there to buy spice. Spice! Their clothes were all neatly folded and stacked in a pile

Alberta Clipper

on the floor. "They all got frozen at the same time," Chambers told me. "Like women who live together and find their menstrual cycles getting in sync." Usually people snap, just rip their clothes off because they're burning up, they're on fire, they're going crazy. For a cop, Chambers had a sense of humor, and he offered his version of the Malaysians' last conversation, complete with the accents: *Are you warm? Yes, very much. I'm very very warm. I believe I'll remove some garments. Yes. I believe I will, also.* And so on. They were found buck naked, sitting upright, waiting patiently for help.

I was still in the shivering stage. I thought about taking off my clothes and folding them up, to make my final act a humorous one, but only Chambers would have gotten the joke. Not Lacey, not Stad, not Eleanor. The wind was really howling. It was the first time I'd actually listened to a blizzard. Normally you have the television on, or the radio. In a vehicle you have the windows up and the sound of the engine, the tires on the road. Even at home with the power out, the sound is tainted by walls and windows, by people talking. It occurred to me that only dead people have really listened to blizzards. In my pickup, with the window partly open, I could hear it clearly. It sounded like a lost dog moaning. I tried to hear it subsiding but it was pretty constant. They'd predicted two days of steady blowing.

Lacey and I went to Nevada for a reason. To conceive. We weren't scientific about it. Weren't trying to get pregnant so bad we'd resorted to specialists or thermometers or anything. But we did think getting away, going somewhere pretty, somewhere relaxing, might be the ticket. It didn't happen in Reno. She never got pregnant again. Maybe her worries about fire had something to do with it, or jet lag, or the champagne we drank like water. Lacey thought it was all the electromagnetic energy from the slots downstairs, filtering up, killing sperm. We had already gone through three miscarriages in as many years. You don't get used to them, to hearing your wife on the phone asking you to please come down to her work place with a change of underwear and some pants because she just lost a baby on her fifteen minute break. If that sounds like a trailer park soap opera, so be it. Real life often does.

People go crazy in crazy situations. Was that why Eleanor let me slip it to her in the kitchen? You hear these stories about

John Salter

crazy people taking charge in a crisis, a flood or war, and being highly effective, until the moment passes and they go back to being crazy. Does the opposite hold true for sane people? This kid me and Stad knew in school, this straight-laced, gung-ho ROTC kid, wound up taking his girlfriend up above Alabama in an Army helicopter and throwing her out. Her crime? She told one of his buddies how he was afraid of squirrels. Squirrels! I wasn't crazy in Stad's bed. That was something I'd thought about doing, not every day but probably once a week at least and for a moment or two whenever I saw Eleanor. We'd never even come close before. We'd gone camping once, the four of us, before Stad and Eleanor had their daughter, Emily. This was back when we were basically newlyweds and children were on the horizon for all of us. Stad and Lacey were playing cards so me and Eleanor went for a walk, a hike. This was up at Lake Itasca, and we wanted to cross the Mississippi on stepping stones, which you could do then, which I'm sure you can still do. I had to help Eleanor over a deadfall and I took the opportunity to press my hand against her bottom, which was only slightly firmer than it is now, almost twenty years later. She gave me kind of a funny look, then, and I know I turned red. But she said nothing about it. Two decades later and we're getting it on. Time! My fingers had gone numb at Itasca and my heart hurt because it wasn't a legal touch, didn't go anywhere, made me want her even more.

The wind swirled around the cab of the pickup and whipped snow into my eyes. When you're freezing to death, you reach a point where your body starts flicking the switch on your different organs, exactly like when your car alternator goes out at night and you kill the radio, kill the heater, do everything you can to keep a trickle of juice to your headlights so you can make it home safely. *Fuck the kidney*, says the heart. *Fuck the spleen.* I'm in charge here.

Stad and I grew apart a little when they had their daughter, Emily. That's not uncommon. Man gets a girlfriend or child and his friends suffer. It hurt us, though, hurt me and Lacey that their baby didn't give up in the womb like all of ours did. We never spoke of it. But once, close to Emily's first birthday, we went shopping at Target for cleaning supplies. I suggested we look for a baby outfit for Emily. I wasn't thinking. I just said it. A little

Alberta Clipper

later, I was pushing the cart, trying to navigate between the racks, and when I looked up, Lacey was holding a tiny dress in both hands. From where I was standing it looked like she was holding a baby, a limp baby. Lacey's hands, rough and strong as mine almost, were shaking. We were surrounded by strollers and cribs and little jackets, shoes, all these things we'd avoided, entire sections of stores that we'd always just hurried by. Stad and Eleanor had said they wouldn't have a kid until they owned a house and when they bought their place, like clockwork, Eleanor got pregnant. She'd never even looked pregnant, she carried it so well. Lacey was pregnant for a grand total of nine months, sick the whole time, her face broken out. The first time, I'd bought some little hiking boots. They were still in my shop, hanging from a peg above my workbench, dried out now, and dusty. I should have thrown them out long ago but you reach a point where you just can't. Why? At Target that night there were dozens of people around. None of them knew our story. They had their own stories. I grabbed Lacey and we left, abandoned our shopping cart, went to a bar and drank beer and ate popcorn and watched the NBA playoffs. We wound up getting Emily a savings bond, I think.

Five hours passed, or five minutes. I remembered the pistol in my coat pocket. If you shoot yourself in the head you won't feel the cold. I took it out, not to kill myself but to eliminate that option. I didn't want to go crazy later and shoot myself and have everyone thinking it was just plain suicide. *He left while I was watching* Terms of Endearment *and drove down the road and shot himself. How bizarre.* How would everyone know I was on the verge of death already? Would they even bother to poke a thermometer into my liver? Would Eleanor blame herself? I took out the Iver Johnson. I was going to throw the revolver out the window, started to wind up, then a little jolt of electricity made it to my brain and I realized it would be more practical to just throw out the ammunition. I had trouble working the catch on the cylinder with my frozen fingers but got it open, shook the cartridges out. They rolled all over the bench seat. I could only find four of them. I jabbed my fingers like a spear into the crack behind the seat but couldn't find the other two cartridges. This was a problem. I was sure that back at the house, standing in front of my closet, I'd checked the revolver, sure I remembered six faded brass circles. I looked at the four in my palm, threw them out the window. Gone

John Salter

forever. Where were the other two? My left eye froze shut. Pictures flashed in my mind. Stad on the floor with a fresh hole in his forehead. Eleanor screaming, running down the hallway. I couldn't see my breath anymore and wondered if I was dead. I thought again of that story, *The Pedersen Kid*. There was a murder in there but it was hard to find. I had to keep going back and rereading. People in the class complained about the writing style. They wanted to know why Gass didn't have to use punctuation marks and they did. The professor got mad. "We'll move on, then," he'd shouted. "On, to Dostoyevsky." It occurred to me that maybe that was the point. In a blizzard things are confusing. Maybe Gass wrote it that way on purpose, used his style to capture the confusion. I wished I'd thought of that in class, had thought to raise my hand and offer it. It would have made a good essay topic. I smelled the revolver like they do in movies, to see if it had been fired. It didn't smell like anything in particular. My crotch hurt. The dampness from being with Eleanor was frozen. You can't imagine how that feels. I saw Eleanor running down the hall. She was so beautiful and I couldn't have her. Stad didn't deserve her. My other eye started to close up.

I saw orange in the window. You hear about people seeing light when they die, but orange? I was sure I'd bought the farm. An angel appeared. The angel was wearing a blaze orange ski mask. I knew that ski mask. It was Lacey's. She was rubbing snow away from the door with her wood-chopper mitts. Then she was jerking the door open, yanking me out of the pickup. My wife! My Lacey, who can peel fifty-pound sacks of dog food from a pallet all day long while the college boys hide out in the break room smoking cigarettes. She carried me like a board to her little Toyota and poked me through the back door. She had the heater going full-blast even though she can't stand being too warm. George Strait was playing on the stereo. I glanced at my pickup as we pulled away. Just a shine of green surrounded by white. Another ten minutes and I might have been there until spring.

All my dreams were of fire. The Eiffel tower burned and melted until it looked like a Salvador Dali painting. My fingers and toes were blowtorches. My privates were a campfire and Stad and Lacey were dangling marshmallows over my crotch.

Alberta Clipper

"Finally," Lacey said.

I looked at her. We were in bed. We were naked. She was watching television. She'd brought the VCR into the bedroom and wired it to the little set we kept on her hope chest to watch the news on, watch David Letterman, check the morning weather. She was sipping Dr. Pepper through a straw. I put my hand on her hip. Warm. Soft.

"Don't get any funny ideas. I'm just trying to defrost you."

"What time is it?"

"Late. You want a little cup of brandy?"

"Yes," I said.

She got up, paused the VCR, and shuffled out with her afghan wrapped around her. I've never seen her naked in her entirety. My thighs were cold. I heard her in the kitchen pouring the brandy. Heard her talking to the cats, filling their water dish. She came back. I sat up. I felt like a stranger. It was the damnedest thing, like I'd been gone for years, in a war. I sipped the brandy. She got back under the covers and stared at me. "How are you feeling?"

"I don't know. Cold."

"Obviously." She laughed.

I nudged closer to her, stealing her warmth. She groaned and adjusted to see the television. I closed my eyes, smelled her. She smelled like Ivory soap. I thought I detected a whiff of Eleanor under the covers and it came back to me, parts of the day, Eleanor's small breasts brushing across my mouth, her earrings scratching my tongue. More: my revolver and the missing cartridges. *Couple murdered during blizzard, suspect a close family friend.* I started to cry. Lacey rubbed my hair. "Now what's wrong?"

"I don't know."

"You're still goofed up. Just rest."

"I'm sorry," I said.

"For what? Being a damned fool?"

"I guess."

She laughed. "You talk nonsense when you're frozen. I wish I'd had a tape recorder. Since when do you want to go to Paris?"

"I don't want to go to Paris."

I heard her take a slurp with her straw. "I called Stad. He'll help you yank out your pickup tomorrow."

"You talked to Stad?"

"He said to tell you if you'd bought a Chevrolet instead of a Ford this wouldn't have happened."

John Salter

"Sounds like Stad."

"Be quiet now. My movie's almost over."

I moved down a little and put my ear against her belly, closed my eyes and listened to her insides rumbling, a tiny ocean, lively enough for me. Her fingers found my hair and we stayed like that while the storm rattled the windows.

About the Author:

John Salter was born in North Carolina, raised in eight states, and educated at the University of North Dakota. The recipient of a McKnight Artist Fellowship, he has worked as a convenience store clerk, directed a California Indian Education Center, taught for three different colleges, and served as Relief Postmaster of Glyndon, Minnesota, where he lives with his family.

Photo by Nancy Salter